TASTES like CANDY

IVY THOLEN

Contact Ivy: ivy@ivytholen.com

Author Photo: Dina Remi – www.dinaremistudios.com

Cover: paulwks – instagram.com/paulwks.art

For Paul,
Obviously.

CHAPTER 1

Mrs. Murphy, my neighbor, perched in the big bay window next to her front door every afternoon to wait for the mail. She's done this as long as I can remember. Even when I was little, it struck me as odd.

"Why does she stare at her mailbox every day?" I asked my mother one day after kindergarten. "Is she waiting for something?"

"Probably," she said, then immediately changed the subject by asking what I wanted for my after school snack.

"Peaches and walnuts," I said.

Peaches and walnuts it was.

A few years later, I asked again.

"Mom, Mrs. Murphy is in the window. Has she been waiting for the same letter for seven years?"

"Please leave that old woman alone, Violet. Worry about yourself." Her voice wavered slightly, just enough for me to drop the subject.

I found out the truth my Freshman year of high school.

Mrs. Murphy waited around for her mail because she had nothing else to do.

Mr. Murphy died before we moved in. They had a son, but

he walked away from their family and didn't visit often. She never left her house, so the only regular human contact she had was from our mail carrier.

"She doesn't have anyone, does she?" I asked my mom.

"No."

"Is that going to be you someday?" I asked. I'd planned to go away to college. She'd raised me alone; my father didn't want to be a dad, and she never had other kids.

"I've got your grandparents, I've got friends, and even if you're gone, you're not going to abandon me, are you?"

I shook my head. "I'll come to visit, and you'll come to visit."

"I don't know if I can handle that horrible Arizona heat," she said, smiling.

Even then, I'd decided to attend Desert Springs University in Phoenix, a small school with one of the best music composition programs in the country. I played violin - first chair since sixth grade - and I wanted nothing more than to write music for movies. As a kid, my favorite film was a cartoon about a kangaroo and a silly sailor called *Story Time*. I ran around singing the theme for years. Annie Wood, the composer, was a DSU alumna. She was my hero; I had no other choice but to follow in her footsteps.

My future was set in stone by kindergarten.

Or so I thought.

Kids in my class started getting college acceptance letters during the spring of our Junior year. The first person was Claire Smithson. Claire was swim team captain, water polo team captain, and softball team co-captain, as well as Vice President of the Student Athlete Association. She got a full-ride scholarship to swim for her first choice school. College was an afterthought for her; she needed a place to train for the Olympics.

Letters really poured in over the summer. Each time I found out another classmate had been accepted, my heart dropped. Desert Springs was the only school I'd applied to, and I hadn't heard a peep. By the time August rolled around, I'd become a full-blown basket case.

That's when I started sitting in my window to wait for the mail.

That's when I became Mrs. Murphy.

Our mail carrier was a friendly lady with curly red hair and gold-rimmed glasses. She would smile and wave as she dropped our mail inside the mailbox mounted next to our front door.

I didn't want to come off as crazy, so I would wave back and wait until she turned her little white mail truck onto the main road. When she disappeared from my sight, I would run to the mailbox, sift through the bills, HEB coupons, and random junk, praying I would find a nice, thick envelope from DSU in the pile.

For a month or two, every time I dug through the envelopes, failure punched me in my gut. I reminded myself it was still early, and Claire got her letter so quickly because schools were fighting over a girl who would surely win a gold medal someday. Other kids got accepted into less competitive schools. My best friend, James, also hadn't gotten her acceptance into Texas A&M. There was nothing to worry about.

Then one day, she did.

"I checked A&M's portal, and I'm in!" she screamed over the phone.

Bile rose in my throat. "Awesome!" I croaked. "Not surprised. So cool! You'll found the next Google, and I will cheer from the dumpster where I live."

James knew me well enough to know my jealousy had nothing to do with her. I knew she wanted to gush and give me all the details about A&M. She held back for my sanity.

"Are you sure it's a letter?" she asked for the hundredth time. "Most schools send acceptances online."

"DSU prides itself in tradition. People I talked to told me I would receive a fancy envelope with gold calligraphy on it. The letter inside is hand-painted on canvas."

"How extra," she said.

"It's suitable for framing," I laughed.

Fast forward to August. I'd stopped laughing by then. Every day I waited for the mail; every day I got another little stab to my heart. Sometimes I cried. Sometimes I acted like a raving bitch to my mom. Sometimes I laid on my bed, shut my eyes, and went numb.

One day, about a week before the first day of our Senior year, as I sat in the window and watched Mrs. Murphy pet her huge Doberman Pinscher, I got a text from James.

JAMES

OMG. Did you get yours?!!!

VIOLET

Course not. I'm not getting in, and they think I'm such a loser they aren't even going to bother rejecting me.

JAMES

Ohhhh. Not that. Sorry. Meant your scavenger hunt invitation. You had to have gotten one. There's no way Maddy didn't pick you.

I sighed. The Senior Scavenge. Of course.

Each year in August, a group of outgoing Senior girls gathers together to plan a scavenger hunt around town for their successors. Invites went to club leaders, girls with perfect GPAs, top athletes, the best and brightest our school had to offer.

Between six and ten incoming Seniors would get an invite and a little poem telling them what item they need to find. It happened the Saturday night before school started. On Sunday morning the incoming Seniors met the outgoing Seniors at Crave Inn for pecan pancakes to celebrate the new school year. Maddy Bryant, who was drum major for Pritchett High's marching band my Junior year, was a good friend and had already told me she'd be giving her invite to me.

For me, the whole thing was a sweet little distraction to stop me from stressing over my acceptance letter for an evening.

Some girls were wildly excited about being chosen. James was one of those girls. She had a hidden rebellious streak and saw the Scavenge as a way to pull off a low stakes heist. Dangerous enough to make her pulse race, not so hazardous that someone might get hurt.

James and I met in sixth grade. We were required to take a music class, and while I fell in love with my violin, James was barely able to hold her viola properly. The simple act of tightening her bow provided expert level physical comedy. She wrapped the horse hair around her arm and pretended to tighten the screw with her teeth. I laughed because she wanted me to, but watching her destroy the bow irritated me so much that I grabbed it from her and did it myself.

"You don't have to help me," she said.

"I can't watch you hold your viola with that weird death grip. I don't have a choice but to help you."

She smiled at me, flashing a mouth full of clear plastic braces.

Once she got her music credit, she quit orchestra, but we remained close.

While I kept up with my violin, she found her groove in STEM classes and became obsessed with coding. During her first year of Computer Science, she blew through an entire semester's reading and tutorials by October. James' teacher was so impressed he helped her create a personal curriculum for the rest of the year. She finished her "rest of the year" school work by February.

He didn't bother creating special projects for her after that.

Instead, he gave her the materials for Computer Science II to earn class credit in time to take Computer Science III Sophomore year.

When I took a basic HTML class, it was her turn to hold my hand. As I struggled to understand CSS, she told me code was another language to learn, just like Spanish or French.

"You like puzzles, right?" she'd asked me.

"Yeah, jigsaw puzzles. This is math. I hate math."

"But unlike geometry proofs, this is math with immediate visual results."

"If I put in the right code, it turns the screen purple. It's an immediate visual result, but a color change doesn't excite me."

"Would a failing grade in Computer Science excite you?"

I saw her point, and she dragged me over the finish line. I got an A, and she got the idea to start a coding club. For James, teaching someone to code was almost as much fun as doing it herself.

We helped each other like this a lot. When James didn't care about something, she ignored it entirely until it came back to bite her in the ass. If not for me needling her, she never would've finished her assigned reading in English. She returned my favor by talking me down from the ledge whenever anxiety paralyzed me.

I needed her pep talks a lot the summer before Senior year.

VIOLET

Mail isn't here yet.

JAMES

Maybe you'll get your invite and your acceptance letter!

VIOLET

Your optimism is appreciated.

Three little dots appeared on my screen as James typed her reply. I watched them blink for a full minute before my phone buzzed.

JAMES

> If I can get into A&M, you're getting into DSU.
> There isn't a doubt in my mind. You've won
> national awards. You toured with the all-state
> orchestra. You got to sit in with the Austin City
> Orchestra for God's sake! Add in your other
> extracurriculars and your GPA and test scores,
> they'd be crazy not to take you. And DO NOT
> give me your "maybe my audition tape sucked"
> bullshit. It was perfect. PER-FECT.

I smiled down at my phone. I loved having my own personal cheerleader.

Then, as if I summoned her, an actual cheerleader reached out.

MILA

> Did you get it?!!!!!!!!!

The text was followed by a selfie of Mila Kelley, grinning from ear to ear, a postcard pressed to her dimpled cheek.

Mila was one of the prettiest girls I'd ever met. Her huge, green eyes always sparkled with mischief, and her friendly demeanor radiated from deep inside. When people spoke to her, she focused all her attention on their words, and she asked lots of questions so you knew she was engaged. It was too intense for me, and I often averted my eyes, lest my awkward self turn to stone from her gaze. She gently mocked me for it. Her teasing made me blush tomato red, which amused her.

She was captain of the cheerleading squad at Pritchett, and she would be cheering with the number one college team in the country after graduation. Mila and her squad weren't your stereotypical rah-rah-pom-pom basic cartwheel types. They were the cheerleaders you could watch on ESPN; she was as much an athlete as Claire.

VIOLET

> Mail hasn't come. James got hers.

MILA

I know. Lolly, Gracie, and River have too. Blythe is far too busy to text me back, but she posted a pic of hers online.

Mila's text came with a gif of Amanda Seyfried doing an epic eye-roll in *Mean Girls*.

VIOLET

We're far less important than her followers, don't you know?

MILA

I know for a fact she almost didn't get an invite. Hannah Tyson had to beg Delilah to send it. Blythe & Delilah went to lunch at El Toro last week. Blythe spent twenty minutes getting a perfect taco salad picture, then she had to craft the perfect self-deprecating caption to make her minions double-tap. Anyway, Remember, Delilah is Miss Manners. She waited until Blythe finished so they could eat together. Hannah said Delilah said she was so hungry she nearly ripped Blythe's tongue out.

VIOLET

Lol.

MILA

You didn't hear this from me, but Delilah told Hannah she would only give Blythe her invite if Blythe did a bunch of chores for her. She like, picked up her dry cleaning and walked her dog. She hand wrote the cards too. How lazy are those bitches if they make us do our own Scavenge invites?

VIOLET

The laziest.

MILA

Indeed.

Blythe Lennon was not an A student. She didn't bother to take the SATs, and she wasn't in any clubs. She didn't like school, and she bitched about all her classes and teachers to ensure we were all well aware of the fact. She wouldn't have even made it to Senior year if her mother hadn't forced her to stay in school.

In Blythe's mind, she didn't need an education.

She was famous.

Her parents split right after they moved to Belldam when Blythe's dad left her mom for her baby brother's nanny. After he left, he decided buying Blythe's love was simpler than coming around to spend time with her. She talked about him like he was a God, and made excuses for him when he went weeks without calling. Watching their relationship unravel made me glad I didn't have a dad.

Their relationship changed the day Blythe discovered YouTube.

She was always a girly girl. When we had sleepovers in junior high, she would bring an overflowing makeup crate and give us all makeovers. Her one shame in life was her embarrassing inability to draw a straight wing with liquid eyeliner. One night I came over to watch her favorite movie, *The Princess Diaries*, for the fiftieth time. While Anne Hathaway got her princess makeover, Blythe sat on the carpet in the middle of her den drawing and redrawing jagged black lines on her right eye.

"Why don't you watch a makeup tutorial?" I asked. "I wanted to learn to curl my hair for when my mom took me to see The Nutcracker. I watched a girl do it on YouTube. It helped me a lot."

She turned to me, her eyes red and swollen. "You can watch someone put on eyeliner?"

"You can watch a lot of people put on eyeliner."

She paused the movie and opened YouTube. "What do I search?"

I suggested 'liquid eyeliner tutorial.' The first hit was a pretty blonde girl with alien eyes. She held up six liquid eyeliner tubes, and the caption promised she would pick the best product and teach you how to use it. We watched her video and learned Urban Decay made the blackest liner, while MAC had the most innovative applicator. I didn't know why either of these things would make it easier to draw a wing, but Blythe was hooked.

When she saw me the next Monday, she ran at me and slammed me into a locker.

"Guess what!" she yelled.

"What?" I asked, struggling to free myself from her death grip.

She closed her eyes, then opened them and batted her lashes. She'd finally done it: two picture-perfect wings, and no broken capillaries.

"Tape!" she screeched. "A girl said to use scotch tape to make a stencil. It worked! Next, I'm going to learn how to contour."

Her dad came around for their quarterly dinner and was surprised at her new skills. She gushed about beauty gurus on YouTube, and he told her she should start her own channel. He bought her a fancy DSLR, a professional quality mic, and a lighting setup. He even consulted with an interior designer to help her decorate her bedroom to use as a backdrop.

At first, being on camera terrified her. She stammered a lot and couldn't clearly explain her techniques. She tried to mimic other girls she'd watched, and she came off as a wannabe. Her dad watched a video where she compared red lipsticks and told her they might need to return her camera.

His words crushed her soul. She cried to James and me, begging for advice on what she'd done wrong.

"It seems so easy for other girls. I don't get it. I'm so fake."

"Yeah," James said. "You are."

Blythe wailed.

"You're not fake," I said, hugging her and stroking her hair.

"She is. Look at her in the nail polish haul. She sounds like a robot. Blythe, you watch these videos, right?"

"Yeah," Blythe said between hiccups.

"Do you watch certain channels more than others?"

"Yeah."

"Why? Are they the best makeup artists?"

Blythe stopped crying. "No. I watch the girls I'd want to be friends with."

James pulled up a video of Blythe on her phone. It had 17 views.

"Do you want to be friends with this girl?" James asked, pointing to her screen.

Then it clicked. Blythe didn't need to learn to be a makeup artist. She needed to develop a character.

Her first big hit was a video entitled, "How to Fake Being a Beauty Guru." In it, she took the cliches all the other girls used and flipped it around to make fun of it. She dropped her Texan accent and began speaking with extreme vocal fry. She drew ten nearly identical red lipstick swatches on her forearm and made jokes about how they were soooooo different. My favorite part was when she cried while putting on eyeliner.

At the end of the video, she dropped the vocal fry and spoke in her normal voice.

"My name is Blythe. I have no idea what I'm doing. If you want to watch me make an ass of myself, like and subscribe."

Her video went viral. People love to watch a pretty girl with a sense of humor screw stuff up.

After Blythe decided to go full goofball, she became an instant success. Three million people watched her accidentally dye her skin green when she added some food coloring to her foundation for Halloween. Five million people watched her bake a cake covered in craft store glitter instead of edible glitter. Ten million people watched a crossover video where she gave a guy from a prank channel a tattoo of Olaf from *Frozen*. Poor Olaf looked more like a dick than a snowman.

"Do you want to build a peeeenisssss?" she sang while she added a snow flurry around Olaf.

Her high view count lured in a slew of sponsors. When millions of people watch your videos, companies hurl tons of junk at you in hopes you'll promote their garbage products. PR reps sent her everything from weight loss tea that nearly made her shit her pants, to weird 'toilet mints' you dropped in before you used the bathroom to cover the poop smell. ("She's going to need those mints if she keeps drinking that nasty tea," Mila once joked. "I went into the bathroom after her…big mistake. It was like a dead animal rotting on a gas station sidewalk in July.")

Eventually, she didn't need her dad's money anymore because she made a killing on YouTube. She still sent him links when new videos went live; the only time they spoke was when she asked him to critique her work.

As Blythe grew more famous, it became harder to be her friend. Stuff we bought, movies we watched, mundane conversations about teachers at school, all of it was potential content for her channel. Eating out with her became a nightmare when she developed a satire series on her blog where she took mediocre food pics and wrote about them as though she were describing a beautiful, gourmet meal. She pissed Mila off when she tried out for cheerleading as a joke for her channel. We got into a huge fight when she ditched my 16th birthday party to fly to LA for a content creator's convention.

Spending a night with Blythe at the Senior Scavenge would be a nightmare.

VIOLET

She's not going to film the whole scavenger hunt, is she? She won't right? Pritchett is pretty boring at night in the dark.

MILA

It's not at Pritchett this year.

VIOLET

What? Hasn't it been at the school since the 80s?

MILA

Yup. I guess the girls wanted to mix things up.
Check my photo.

I scrolled back to examine the pic of Mila's invite. The front image showed a row of demonic clown heads, their gaping mouths waiting for someone to fill their gullets with water to inflate the orange balloons on their pointy black hats.

VIOLET

The Carnival?!

MILA

Guess so. How cool is that?

In theory, it was awesome. The Poison Apple Halloween Carnival was Belldam's premier year-round tourist attraction for families. It was a creepy amusement park where all the rides and attractions were Halloween themed. Visitors could spin in giant Crazy Cauldrons in a rip off of Disney's teacup ride, or sit inside rotting bugs on the little kid's Black Kitten Coaster, or win little stuffed werewolves and mummies as prizes on the midway. There were special events and performances, too; Mila had performed in a zombie gymnastics show the year before.

In practice? The carnival creeped me out, and the idea of wandering around its empty carnival grounds in the dark made me want to hide in my closet until my mom dragged me out on the first day of school.

VIOLET

Can't we get in trouble?

MILA

Dude, that's why it's so fun.

I pulled the sheer curtain back from my window and looked out to see our mail carrier walking toward my house. I tossed my phone on my couch and ran to greet her.

"Hi, Misty!" I said. "How's it going?"

"Hot," she chuckled as she handed me a fat stack of papers with a FedEx bubble mailer on top.

"Good luck keeping cool! And thank you!"

Misty nodded. "Hope you got what you're waiting for, sweetie."

Back inside, I dumped the pile on our kitchen counter. The package belonged to my mom, some random thing she ordered online. Ten different envelopes advertised how she'd been approved for various credit cards. I knew if you got those, your credit was good. I mumbled, "Yay for you, mom," as I sorted the envelopes for recycling. A state senate candidate smiled awkwardly up at me from a massive red, white, and blue mailer. He promised he would improve the lives of all Texans by exterminating all the weasels in Austin. He did not identify the weasels, nor elaborate on how he would banish them from the Capitol.

His mailer went straight into the bin.

At the bottom was a teal envelope addressed to me. I turned it over, and a peacock doodle waved at me from the sealed flap. I ripped the peacock in two and pulled out my scavenger hunt invitation. I set it aside to sort through the other mail a second time.

No matter how many times I shuffled through the mail, my acceptance letter never appeared.

I took my scavenger hunt invite to the couch and dramatically fell face-first into the cushions. A huge Beistle style jack o' lantern grinned at me from the center of the Ferris wheel. Each black gondola had a similar cartoon painted on the side: ghosts, black cats, spooky owls. Orange lights lining the wheel glowed orange against an inky blue sky. It was the ultimate

Halloween ride, as picture-perfect in real life as it was on the card in my hand.

Twice a year or so, my friends and I made a trek out to the carnival. The massive Whirling Witch Coaster and the Ferris wheel were the only rides I'd never ridden. Heights scared me to death, and I wasn't one of those people who liked being frightened on purpose. James thought I was crazy.

"The gondolas aren't even open!" she laughed. "You're locked in a cage. You can't fall out!"

It didn't matter. Fantasies filled my brain, straight from the handful of horror movies I'd watched. Cracked, rusty hinges could cause gondolas to snap free. You could be locked in with a deadly wasp. The whole thing could get struck by lighting. It was, after all, the tallest Ferris wheel in Texas, a perfect lightning rod.

I turned my card over to read Blythe's pretty orange handwriting on the back.

THE POISON APPLE HALLOWEEN CARNIVAL
AUGUST 29
MIDNIGHT

CONGRATULATIONS, CHOSEN GIRL
JUMP UP AND DOWN, DO A TWIRL
WALK THE GROUNDS AND FOLLOW THE GRASS
FROM THE RIDE ENTRANCE
STEAL A PASS.

MEET YOUR MAKERS AT THE CRAVE INN AT SUNRISE.
HOPE YOU LIKE PECAN PANCAKES!!!

Beneath the printed message, Maddy had signed her name in black ink and had drawn eight bubbly hearts. I snapped a picture of both the Ferris wheel and the poem and sent it to James.

VIOLET

Thoughts?

She replied with her own poem. It read:

JAMES

Wet and wild, darling child

A fish tank with no fish

Bring us a sphere stitched with red

Be warned

You may need to hold your breath.

Whatever that meant, it made my heart race a bit for her. James was petrified of water. She didn't even like to take baths. If she were required to swim to get her item, it would likely be me diving in to retrieve it.

JAMES

You have to get a Ferris wheel fast-pass. I have to swipe a baseball from the dunk tank.

She sent me a pic, and sure enough, the flip side was an artsy dunk tank shot.

VIOLET

Weren't these clues supposed to be mind bending puzzles?

JAMES

Guess the hard part is breaking into the carnival without getting caught. When the Scavenge was at the school, the girls told the principal ahead of time. Maybe they have the same arrangement with the carnival?

Fat chance. The Eaton family, rich jerks who acted like they owned the whole town when they only owned most of it, owned the carnival. No way would they permit anyone - especially not unsupervised teenage girls - to roam free on their property after hours. But if believing we had permission for the Scavenge gave James peace, who was I to destroy her bad girl burglary fantasy?

My mother got home from work surprisingly early that night.

She was an events coordinator at the Belldam Tower Hotel, the hottest spot in town for weddings in the spring and summer. I'd barely seen her since May, but no one wanted to get married in Texas in late August, so she "only" had to work 60 hour weeks by then.

She knew better than to ask out loud if I'd gotten my DSU acceptance letter. At first, right after I applied, she would come home with wide, hopeful eyes, waiting for good news. The longer I waited, the more she pretended to ignore my anxiety. Eventually, it seemed like she gave up altogether.

She dropped her laptop bag on the kitchen counter next to the spot where I'd left my invitation to the Scavenge. She picked it up and read both sides.

"What's this?" she asked.

"Senior Scavenge."

"Oh fun," she said. She meant it with genuine happiness; I took it as sarcasm.

"It's whatever. I have to steal a fast-pass from the carnival. It'll take ten minutes."

She ignored my tone. "Who else got an invitation?"

"People you'd expect. James, Mila, Blythe, Lolly. I haven't talked to her, but I'm sure Claire Smithson. Lolly told Mila that Gracie Scott and River Ellis got one too."

"Which ones are they?"

"You met Gracie at Arts Night. She's the girl who draws a web comic called *Graceful River* that got bought by a real publishing company. She's got short black hair with blunt bangs."

"And the glasses too big for her face?"

"Yeah, huge round glasses. River is her partner. She writes the comics. She's a major stoner, dresses super prim and proper so you'd never know."

My mom dug through her bag. She wasn't looking for anything. She was trying to act nonchalant so she could sound aloof when she asked if I ever hung out with River.

Translation: Is my daughter a stoner too?

"I'm not high right now," I said, one eyebrow raised.

"There's nothing wrong with it. I'd much rather you smoke than drink if you have to do something. Maybe wait to experiment with it in college. And you never, ever drive after."

I rolled my eyes. I had, in fact, smoked with River before at a party, and I hated it. Being high was kind of cool, but the smell was gross, and it made my lungs hurt. Another time, James traded her neighbor some weed chocolate for a bunch of pirated movies. We each ate a piece and watched old Disney cartoons in her attic for hours. I had way more fun with James, but I wasn't about to tell my mom. I wasn't an addict and didn't want to do it more than occasionally. It was pointless to make her worry.

"I'm not stupid enough to drink, do drugs, or text while I'm driving," I said firmly. "I'm a bad enough driver as it is."

She nodded and got some cold rotisserie chicken from the fridge. She asked if I wanted some, I said I'd already made and eaten mac and cheese with broccoli.

"How did I get lucky enough to have a kid who voluntarily eats her veggies?" she asked.

I shrugged and rubbed two fingers together. I'd built up calluses so thick that I barely had any feeling in my fingertips.

"I haven't even started tonight's practice yet," I said. "Gonna go get it done."

"Alright," she said, then paused. "You're an amazing player, Violet. Do you get that? No matter what some stupid school in the middle of the desert thinks. I always pictured you in New England somewhere anyway. You've got your big sweater collection. You wouldn't have a use for them in Phoenix."

The inability to wear sweaters was a strange mark to put in the "Reasons Why Desert Springs Sucks" column, but at least she tried.

I told her thanks, then disappeared into my room. The phrase "no matter what" bounced around in my brain. It felt like a consolation prize, like she was already resigned to my rejection from DSU. I sprawled out on my bed, and instead of picking up my violin, I gripped my pillow.

At some point, I fell asleep. James and Blythe dressed as clowns swimming in a neon green ocean. The wind whipped Blythe's rainbow wig off. It skimmed the water before a wave rushed past, sucking it into the depths.

I stood on the shore, begging James to come back. She waved for me to come in and join them. She didn't see the pair of huge, gloved hands rise from the water to pull her beneath the surface. I screamed for Blythe to save James.

She just swam away.

CHAPTER 2

Every morning my phone woke me up at 5:30.

I had my ringer set to a horrible sound that blared like an alarm at a nuclear power plant mid-meltdown. It's the only one I wouldn't sleep through. I kept it across my bedroom, on a bookshelf, so I would be forced to wake up and move my body to silence the digital screams.

My eyes usually weren't even open. I'd leave my room, head upstairs, realize I had to pee, pee, head back upstairs, and pull out my violin to practice.

I'd sit in my chair, my fingers moving on muscle memory for the first fifteen minutes. Then the light stopped hurting my eyes, and my ears decided to participate. My brain fired up, my heart thumped happily in my chest. I don't drink coffee; I've never needed it thanks to my morning practice session.

This was my routine every single morning without fail.

This is what I loved to do.

My first violin was a loaner from Cedar Bayou Junior High. There was a small chunk missing from the scroll, and the chin rest was dull from decades of preteen facial oils rubbing off its shiny finish. It fell out of tune a lot, and at the time, I didn't know how to fix it, so my orchestra director Priscilla had to spend five minutes before class every day fixing it for me. I didn't care. I loved that violin, warts and all.

Priscilla was a stocky woman, maybe 35 at most, but she was firmly stuck in another decade. She wore baggy sweaters, flared jeans, and had an honest to God mullet. Her oversized, square glasses looked like they belonged to a woman three times her age.

All the kids thought she was dorky. I thought she was sweet. She was the first person to nurture my desire to become a professional musician, the first person to make me believe it was a real possibility.

She's also the one who saved me from the bass.

On the first day of sixth grade, fifteen kids filed into the orchestra room. It had half the footprint of the band hall and was twice as cluttered because Priscilla had a hoarding problem. Cello racks and stacks of instrument cases lined the walls, making the room appear even smaller. None of the chairs matched. Priscilla had to steal them from different places around the school: low, plastic blue from the cafeteria, narrow cream wood from an English class, rickety folding chairs from the auditorium, stools from a Biology lab. Orchestra was the raggedy little sister of band and choir, an afterthought class with a minuscule budget.

But Priscilla made it work.

"You can choose whatever instrument you want, whatever speaks to you. Violins sit on the far right, violas next to them, cellos on the end. Bass players are in the back. We have a harp too. Not for any of you, only eighth graders can learn harp. It's something you have to progress to."

Everyone shuffled to their seats.

Everyone except me.

My mom made the mistake of showing me *Jaws* at the ripe old age of four. Fortunately, I didn't develop a water phobia, but I did become obsessed with the theme song. I bellowed out the deep notes - *duuun dun, duuun dun* - and bolted around the house, bent at the waist with my arm sticking up to approximate a shark fin. I'd run straight at her and butt her legs with my head while continuing the theme.

One day she told me the instrument that made that sound was a standup bass.

I yammered about it all summer to anyone who would listen.

"I'm going to play the bass," I told my dentist.

"I watched videos of people playing bass for hours last night," I told the waitress at Chili's.

"A bass' rumble is probably the prettiest sound in the world," I told a man on my front lawn as his dog peed on my mother's marigolds.

When the big day rolled around, and I stood next to a trio of big basses, I was intimidated. I hadn't yet hit my growth spurt, my arms were weak sticks.

My heart pounded in my chest.

Duuun dun. Duuun dun.

"Sweetie, what's your name?" Priscilla asked.

"Violet," I whispered.

"Do you know what you want to play?"

"Bass?"

Her forehead crinkled. "I'm so sorry," she said, her voice soft. "I might not have one in your size. Come here, let's check."

She pulled the smallest bass off the rack and stood it next to me. Despite its relatively diminutive size, it was still way too big for me. She handed me the neck, and it swayed, nearly knocking me over.

"It's too big," I said.

"No shit," laughed a boy with white-blonde hair. His name was Troy, and later he would become my first boyfriend. We dated for exactly one week before he moved to Canada without saying goodbye.

Priscilla put the bass back on the rack.

"What's the best part about orchestra?" she asked, not pausing long enough for me to answer. "If you can play one of these instruments, you can play them all. We can start you out on violin or viola, and when you're a little taller, you can switch."

I sighed. "Okay," I said. "Violin, I guess."

She ushered me to an empty seat in the front row, right next to a girl with curly red hair pulled back into a tight ponytail. She wore a green army jacket that swallowed her skinny frame.

"I'm James," she said. She extended a hand. Chipped black polish flecked her nails. I wasn't allowed to wear anything except clear.

"Do sixth graders shake hands?" I asked.

She jerked her hand back. It disappeared deep into her sleeve. "We don't have to."

I smiled. I slid my fingers up James' sleeve, found her fingers, and pulled her hand out to shake it.

"Gay," said Troy.

James turned around in her seat and looked him in the eye. "Is that a problem?" she asked. "My dad is gay. Is there something wrong with my dad?"

Troy's eyes bulged. The color drained from his face, and he sputtered out an apology.

James turned around, smirking.

"Is your dad really gay?" I asked.

"Nope." She grinned, flashing me her metal filled mouth.

Priscilla spent the rest of the class doling out instruments and logging serial numbers to track them if one went missing. She started in the back, with Troy and his bass. When she handed James her viola, James promptly dropped it on the floor, butter side down. Priscilla screeched and dove to rescue it. Fortunately, the viola wasn't damaged. Their relationship, however, wasn't as lucky. Priscilla could barely hide her disdain for James from then on.

Finally, Priscilla presented me with a navy blue rectangular case. I unzipped it on my lap, careful not to drop it. I lifted the violin from the stiff velvet and placed it under my chin.

"It's a little dented," she said. "Eighth graders get the good ones. It's still good."

It smelled like pennies. I plucked the E string, and the shrill sound made me jump.

"It's so shrill," I said.

"Wait until you play it with a bow," Priscilla said with a wink.

Priscilla didn't require us to take our instruments home. I did anyway. At home, I placed the case on the dining room table. My mother tilted her head.

"Isn't it a little small for a bass?" she asked.

"I changed my mind."

"Violin?"

"Violin."

I took it out, tightened the bow, and rubbed it over the strings in a mad fury.

"Oh God, Violet, you can't make that racket in here," my mom said.

She sent me to my room. I pretended to play, taking extra care to make the E string scream in pain.

The phone rang. Minutes later, my mom knocked on my door.

"Steve Morris next door called. You're scaring his cat. Maybe it's time to put it away."

I'd waited for years to get an instrument in my hands. Stopping wasn't an option.

I considered hiding in my closet amongst my sweaters and

the stuffed animals I was too old to own, yet too young to throw away. Then I remembered the attic.

When our house was built, the initial plans included a second story. Somewhere along the way, the family who built it ran out of money and decided to leave it unfinished. The floor was plywood stacked on beams, insulation was exposed, and there were no windows or air conditioning. A single lightbulb hung from the ceiling, it's light too weak to reach the corners.

The attic scared me to death. I was sure rats, ghosts, or both lived up there. Still, it was tucked away above the guest bathroom, and the walls were thick enough that sound wouldn't travel outside. I shut my eyes, climbed the stairs, and flicked on the light.

My mom bought a chair and a music stand. I situated them directly under the yellow bulb. I sat under my makeshift spotlight and made the violin scream in pain.

At that moment, for the first time, I felt alive.

I never thought about the bass again.

Over the next few years, I spent hours in the attic, sweating my ass off, learning to turn the screams into actual music. Since the violin sounded like a cat, I named him Cheshire after the cat in *Alice in Wonderland*.

I learned each piece Priscilla gave me, then sought out sheet music online and taught myself my favorite film scores: *Beauty and the Beast*, *Lord of the Rings*, and *Psycho*, whose violin screech rivaled *Jaws* for the best horror theme ever. Even as I got older and Priscilla offered me one of the less abused instruments, I kept Cheshire, holding him tight like another limb.

When I graduated from the eighth grade, my mom and Priscilla cried as they gifted me with my very own violin. This one smelled like fresh lacquer, and the back was so shiny I could see my hazy reflection. I cried too…for my ugly old Cheshire. He had been my baby, my teacher, my best friend, next to James.

"I love the new one," I said, gulping for air. "But I'll miss Cheshire. Can I please keep him?" I gripped my old violin close and sobbed.

My mom clucked her tongue, clearly a little offended. The new violin cost a pretty penny. Priscilla, on the other hand, was touched.

"I remember your first day," she said. "Most kids come in, they have fun during class, but practicing at home is a chore. You marched in ready to learn. You really love playing. Now, we could let you sneak out with the old violin, or you could think about the next Violet."

"What?" I asked.

"A new student will start the sixth grade next year. They might be in orchestra to get a music credit, or maybe they'll love music as much as you do. This ugly old thing is probably the most beautiful instrument the school owns because you've poured years of love into it. You can pass him on and pass on your love to another child."

"What kind of hippy bullshit?" mumbled my mom under her breath.

Priscilla's hippy bullshit worked, though. I held him out and allowed her to take him. She went into her office and reappeared with a sticker and sharpie. I watched her scribble on the sticker and saw it was a "Hello, my name is…" name tag. She'd written Cheshire in block letters. She stuck it on the case, zipped it away, and placed it on top of her piano.

"I'll take care of this," she said. "You take care of yourself. Promise?"

"Promise," I said, the tears on my face now coming from pure happiness.

I named my new violin Katniss to keep the cat theme. I spent two hours each morning and three hours at night in the attic with her. She was prettier than Cheshire, her sound richer, and I grew to love her as much as I'd loved him.

On the morning of the Scavenge, my alarm went off as usual. I carried Katniss upstairs and spent the morning playing *Is She With You?*, Wonder Woman's theme from *Batman vs. Superman*. It was a decent session, not perfect, not anything to cry over.

When my 7:30 alarm – marked GET OUTTA THE ATTIC AND BE A HUMAN – went off, I hit snooze and grumbled at myself.

"You wonder why you didn't get into DSU? Mediocrity."

I accidentally bumped Katniss against my music stand, knocking it over. I gasped and examined her to make sure she was okay. When I didn't find any broken parts, I gave one of the pegs a turn, twisted a little too hard, and snapped the E string. It popped against my left index finger, slicing it open.

Blood dribbled from my finger onto the lining of Katniss' case.

"Goddamn it," I mumbled.

I slipped Katniss back in her case and carried her downstairs to search for a bandaid. I wrapped a Hello Kitty bandaid tightly around my finger to stop the bleeding. It went numb, and the tip turned white.

My phone, which was next to the sink, buzzed.

JAMES
U up?

VIOLET
U know it.

JAMES
Done practicing?

VIOLET
Yeah. Why?

JAMES

Take a shower.

VIOLET

No. Why?

JAMES

Get ready, loser. We're going shopping.

CHAPTER 3

When I didn't automatically respond to her text, James called me.

"You are not going to sit around and wait for the mail all day today," she said. "My mom is dragging me to Austin to pick up some boxes from my grandfather, and you're coming with us. After we get back, we're going to dinner with the other girls. Pack whatever you need for today and tonight because you won't be back home until after breakfast on Sunday."

"I promised my mom I'd go through my old clothes to see if anything can be donated," I protested. "And I said I'd mow the backyard."

James laughed. "You don't give a shit about either of those things, and neither does your mom. Take a damn shower. We'll be there soon."

James and her mom Heather pulled into my driveway in their black minivan just as I was tying my shoes. I checked to make sure my ID and debit card were in my phone case and shoved it in my pocket. I debated bringing a hoodie in case it got cold later, but decided against it. James would have her old green jacket, now a perfect fit and covered with pins and patches, I could steal if I needed warmth.

"I'd rather freeze than drag an unworn hoodie around all night," I said to myself.

James flung herself onto my porch and screamed.

"It's Senior Scavenge Day!!!!"

She body slammed me onto the hedges.

"Okay!" I yelled, holding my hands up in surrender. "It's Senior Scavenge Day! I'm excited!"

Honestly, for the first time, I was excited about the Scavenge, after days of wishing I could find a way to skip it.

"What did you do to your hand?" James asked, grabbing me by the thumb.

"Katniss bit me."

"That bitch!"

Heather leaned on her horn and waved us to the car.

"Y'all can scream at each other while we drive," she said when we climbed into the van.

"It's Senior Scavenge!" James screamed.

"Yaaahhhhhhhhhh!" Heather growled, her fingers in a "rock on" gesture.

As a teenager, Heather had purple hair and a nose ring. She went to concerts of bands her parents hated, got drunk, and stumbled in at dawn. She staged an anti-meat protest at her school, complete with gallons of fake blood sprayed on the cafeteria walls. She dated a boy with a lime green mohawk and a self-administered tattoo of a melting skull on his forearm.

All the adults told her she'd be dead by 20 if she didn't change her ways.

Now she was pure soccer mom, in pastel polos with a blunt bob. She married Mohawk Guy, who grew out his hair and spent big money getting his tattoo covered by a professional artist.

Now when Mr. Parker rolls up his sleeve, he's got a bouquet of purple Heliotrope on his arm.

It was James' favorite flower, the same color as her mother's hair when they first met.

Though Heather fully embraced her new mom life, when we went on road trips, a little bit of her old self shone through. On the morning of the Scavenge, we drove to Austin while blasting music from back in Heather's glory days, screaming along with Marilyn Manson and Hole. She made the van move faster than a grocery getter ever should, and when we were on the open road, she put it on cruise control and rested a bare foot on her window.

"Mama," asked James, her voice quiet. "Is it safe to drive with your leg up?"

Heather sheepishly put her foot back on the floor, turned down the music a touch, and announced we were stopping at Torchy's for breakfast tacos.

James rolled her eyes in the rearview.

I sat back, smiling, and squeezed my injured finger.

James' grandfather was selling their old house so he could move to be closer to his daughter's family. The boxes were a mixture of Heather's old junk and her deceased mother's dishes, photo albums, and Christmas ornaments.

"Ninety percent is going in the garbage," James said under her breath as we stuffed everything in the back of the van.

"It's the ten percent that counts," I said.

James sneered. "Then you can come over and help her sort out that ten percent. Oooh. Here's a whole box of notes she and her best friend passed each other in high school."

James lifted the lid off a Doc Martens shoebox, and sure enough, a hundred little folded pieces of paper were stuffed inside. I pulled one out and read the first sentence aloud.

"We should go to Lone Star Mall next weekend and yell at

those tiny stop signs." I frowned and folded the note into a triangle. "Your mom was really weird."

"*Is* really weird," James corrected me. "Look at this one. It's written backward. I could only read this if I held it up to a mirror. My Godmother seriously had way too much time on her hands."

"Do you ever wish you lived back in the 90s? Before phones and stuff?"

"Uh, no. I'd die if I didn't have my phone. We wouldn't have internet, and I'd probably die of boredom without a computer to screw around with. What if there was an emergency or something? Don't romanticize the good old days, especially when you never lived them."

"Fair."

Heather approached us, a plastic tub packed with photo albums under her arm. "We had computers and cell phones in the 90s. We even had the internet. Did I ever tell you girls about AOL?"

James' eyes bulged. "Run," she said and bolted for the house.

I followed her.

James' grandfather, Jimmy, had a garage sale and pawned his belongings off on his neighbors when he decided to sell his house. Two brown velour recliners and a television were the only things left in his living room. We found him in one of the chairs, watching MSNBC.

James sat in the other chair, squishing herself into the corner so I could fit too. The recliner threatened to flip backward, Jimmy told us to settle down.

"I keep waiting for it to rain," he said. "Never does. They say next week it's going to hit a hundred and ten."

Heather swept through the room, checking to see if she'd missed anything.

"Dad, you're not old enough to bitch about rain."

"I'll bitch about whatever I want."

"I hate rain," said James. "I wish it was this hot and sunny all year long."

"Violet, you're going to school in Arizona, right?" asked Jimmy. "James should've gone with you there instead of A&M. Damn Aggies."

My heart stopped. James flicked her eyes in my direction and winced.

"Grandpa, Dad had me in an Aggie blanket at the hospital the day I was born. No way would I go anywhere else. Anyway, Violet hasn't gotten her letter yet. She doesn't know if she's going to Arizona."

I dug an elbow into her ribs. This was the situation where you lie: "*Yes sir, she should've come with me, ha ha ha. Guess she'll have to visit!*"

Jimmy, to his credit, didn't flinch. His eyes remained straight ahead, gaze fixed on a commercial for life insurance.

"Aw, you're going," he said. "Didn't you say they do the letters fancy by hand? Takes more time than to email someone. You'll get in. Not if, when."

"You remembered that DSU sends handwritten letters?" I asked.

"Course. I've only listened to you crow about music school for the past decade."

"Grandpa," said James. "You've only known her for six years."

Jimmy rocked his recliner, using momentum to get to his feet. "Same difference," he said to James. He turned toward the front door, threw back his head, and screeched. "Heather! You done?"

For the first time since we'd gotten to Jimmy's house, Heather was empty handed.

"Yeah, Dad," she said, dusting off her hands. "That's about it."

Jimmy nodded and flopped back into the chair.

"Well, y'all get outta here. Cowboys are fixing to kick the

Texans asses." He turned to us and smiled. "Want you girls to come visit me at my new house though. Right?"

"Course, Grandpa," said James. She crawled out of our chair and into his lap to squeeze him.

Heather and I hugged Jimmy too, then we piled back into the van.

James noted that we still had tons of time, and Heather didn't want to head home yet, so we stopped at Waterloo records to check out the vinyl. She bought James an Elton John album Jimmy had recommended, and even though I said no, she got me the *Beetlejuice* soundtrack.

"I saw that movie in theaters," she said.

"Jesus, Mom. How old *are* you?" James howled.

"Someday," Heather shook her head. "Someday you'll be my age and your daughter will ask you about being old. You'll see."

Heather flipped through a stack of used records and gasped.

"What?" I asked.

She pulled out a copy of Nine Inch Nails' album *The Downward Spiral* and hugged it to her chest.

"I loved this album in high school. I remember my Senior year, I had it on cassette, and I listened to it on a loop when I drove to visit your dad at A&M. I had the biggest crush on Trent Reznor."

James tapped out something on her phone and laughed.

"He's a gross old man! He's like, grandpa's age!"

Heather shook the album at her daughter. "Trent Reznor is *not* Grandpa's age," she said, disgusted at her child's taste in men. "And I had a crush on him when he was young and hot. He's *still* handsome if you ask me."

"I absolutely did not ask you if you thought some puffy old goth was hot," said James. "Violet, did you ask?"

36

I shielded myself with *Beetlejuice*. "Please exclude me from this narrative."

James whipped out her phone and waved it in my face. "I'm going to text your mom and ask her who she had a crush on and if she still thinks he's hot now," she threatened.

"She already told me," I said. "Bill Clinton."

Heather snorted so hard she choked.

CHAPTER 4

Heather needed to pee, so we stopped at a Buc-ee's. She hit the bathroom while James and I got buckets of Dr. Pepper Icees. James took a big swig and squealed.

"Sugar high or brain freeze?" I asked.

"Por que no los dos?" she asked.

We paced the aisles, spying on the other patrons.

A short, round, blonde woman stood at the checkout with an extra large gas station nacho plate in her hand and a baby balanced on her hip. The baby reached for the nachos, grabbing a handful of electric orange cheese sauce. She shoved her entire hand in her mouth and sucked her fingers clean. The woman didn't flinch.

"Babies can have nacho cheese?" I asked.

"Well, you see, Little Addison there has the same constitution as a frat boy," James said, speaking through her nose and using the generic first name she gave all obnoxious children. "Cheese goo, cold pizza, week-old Chinese. Trans fats give her power."

Little Addison gagged, and a cheese shower sprayed down her pink onesie.

"She really is a frat boy," I said.

James rolled her eyes and took another hit off her Icee.

"Do you feel weird?" she asked.

I lifted my drink. "I'm not drinking mine until it's paid for because I'm not a criminal."

"No, not the Icee. About tonight. And next week. And the whole year. Tonight is the beginning of the end. First, it's the Scavenge, then school starts, and we're Seniors, and before you know it we're married to men with beards, and we're wearing yellow polo shirts, peeing every five minutes because the bladder suspensions we got after our hysterectomies left us unable to hold it for more than fifteen minutes."

Her voice got faster and faster until she gasped for air. When she finished, she looked at me, her face blank.

"Oh," I said. I was familiar with James' tone. She stood on the knife's edge of a panic attack and needed me to talk her down. "You've got a pretty specific future mapped out. I guess I'm taking it one day at a time?"

James shook her head. "You know those notes we found?" she asked.

"Heather's? The ones in the shoebox?"

"Yeah. My Godmother Leslie wrote them. They haven't seen each other in like eight years. My mom told me they don't talk much anymore, either."

"Did they fight?"

"No. They used to talk daily, and then they texted, then they just...stopped. Isn't that strange?"

James cradled her cup like Little Addison's mother cradled her baby. It left a dark green wet spot on her jacket between a PRITCHETT PEACOCKS, CLASS OF 2021 patch, and a heart-shaped enamel pin with the phrase DROP DEAD written in the center. She squeezed her eyebrows together, making a pinched scowl.

"It won't happen to us," I assured her.

"We say that," she said. "But...what if it is?"

James wanted me to give her a big speech to make her feel

better about growing up. Though she'd spent as many years waiting for her chance to run away from Belldam as me, lately she spoke like she might be pumping the brakes.

But I didn't have a speech for her. I felt as lost as she did, maybe more. At least she'd gotten into college.

"It won't be," I promised. "A&M isn't far from Belldam. Heather is going to give you her van. You'll drive home, I'll hitchhike and stay in your dorm."

"You're seriously talking like you won't go to school," she said.

"Well, I didn't apply anywhere else because I'm an idiot."

"You're not an idiot. You have a dream. You know why I'm going to A&M? Because my dad went there. I didn't choose my choice. Dad chose it for me in the womb." She bit her bottom lip. "We should get beef jerky."

She bolted for the jerky rack and pulled a few bags off. She ripped a bag of Sweet and Spicy open with her teeth and shoved her face inside. She nipped at the dried meat but couldn't grab any. I took the bag from her, pulled a strip out, and held it for her to bite. Her eyes were watery, and not from the spicy jerky.

"Please don't cry," I begged. "You cry, I'll cry."

"It's the last first day of school."

"Not today it's not. Today is party time! We're breaking into a carnival with all our friends. Don't you wonder what it's like when it's dark and empty? Don't you wonder if maybe ...it's haunted?"

"Everything in Belldam is," she said, jerky gluing her teeth together.

"Evil clowns," I said.

"A psycho killer security guard," she grinned. "Or the Eaton family ghosts, pissed we're getting into the carnival for free."

"Lolly will probably chicken out," I said.

"We'll drag Little Miss Hall Monitor in and feed her fried Coke."

"Do you think they have fried Coke just lying around, ready to eat?"

"We'll find the batter and fry it ourselves!"

"We don't know how to deep fry food!"

James held out the bag and offered me some jerky. I declined.

"I wouldn't call fried Coke food," I said. "I wouldn't call the jerky you're shoving into your gaping maw food either."

"Claire is going to dump Chelle," James said, changing the subject at lightning speed. "She's taking her to see a movie at the Brunson Theater, and then she's setting up a picnic at Roseland Park. She's going to give her the chop while they feed the ducks."

I gasped. Claire and Chelle had been together since homecoming our Sophomore year. Our principal was an ass about two girls going to the dance together, so instead they ditched it and saw *Xylophone Man 2018* at the Brunson and made out in the park after.

"Did she tell you that?" I asked.

"Mila did. Isn't it gross she's recreating their first date?"

"I guess. Why is she doing it?"

"Claire wants to be single for Senior year. All those away games."

I gasped and clutched fake pearls. "Such a slut." An older woman with a stiff bouffant walked past, frowning at my language. I smiled sweetly and whispered to James: "We should watch *Hairspray* tomorrow."

"Oh man, we should watch both *High School Musical* and *Hairspray*. Zefron double feature."

"Remember when they basically forced Gracie to be Tracy Turnblad in the school musical because she was the only big girl who could sing?"

"Yeah."

"Did you know the play traumatized her so badly she went to fat camp the next summer?"

James laughed. "I did *not*. That's how she lost all the weight?"

"Mmmhmm. She told me on the trip to Corpus. You should've come."

"I'd sooner die than be so close to a major body of water. Besides, I had a lovely time in Michigan at my great aunt's funeral that weekend instead."

"You could've missed the funeral of the woman you never even met and stayed on the sand."

"Listen, one minute you're on the sand, the next minute, a current sucks you up and sends you out to King Triton."

"Okay, loser," I said, smiling and shaking my head.

Across the store, Heather emerged from the bathroom. She strained on her tiptoes, surveying the store for us. I hit James' shoulder and pointed at her mother.

"It's time, huh?" James asked. She turned to walk away.

I stopped her.

"This is going to be awesome," I assured her. "Don't waste tonight worrying about tomorrow. Look, I'm smiling!" I stuck my fingers in my mouth and stretched the skin wide. "If Mail Girl can smile, so can you."

"You have gas station hands," she said, hitting me back.

"I'm building immunities," I said, shrugging.

James sucked on her Icee, loud and wet.

"Set our hearts in tune with thee, Violet," she said, speaking our school song's first line.

"Let wisdom be our light, James," I replied with the second line.

"Let my ass be our light, dude."

James lifted her leg and farted at me.

The stiff haired old lady gasped in the next aisle.

I almost peed my pants laughing.

Heather paid for our snacks.

The van hit the road.

Somewhere in Belldam, a man named Ted reported to work.

CHAPTER 5

Ted told people he took his job at the Poison Apple Halloween Carnival to get health insurance. This was a lie. Though nerve damage kept him from feeling his left upper thigh, and some semi-regular chest pains scared him, he refused to see a doctor. If you never find out you're sick, you can't die…right?

In truth, he became a security guard for Eaton Industries because he was lazy. He'd worked for their resort hotel for years, then when he got too old to eject rowdy or nonpaying guests, they transferred him to the carnival. Eight hours a night, in a squishy office chair, a stack of true crime novels by his side. A dream job for a man with no interest in exerting any energy at work.

The late August heat made him lazier than usual. They closed the carnival for a week for pre-Halloween maintenance, so most of the staff were on vacation. Ted worked the evening shift, 3 p.m. to 3 a.m. He was supposed to walk the perimeter twice a night, several miles on foot made difficult by his numb leg. No one ever supervised him, no one really cared. Some nights, when the air was so hot it felt like inhaling fire, he didn't bother to leave his security booth at all.

Sally at the library suggested he read up on the Texas Killing Fields. Thirty young women murdered and left by I-45 down South. Ted didn't

45

have a violent bone in his body, he never could understand how one person could snuff the light out of another person's eyes.

His ex-wife got him into true crime. She read the books because she wanted to be prepared in case someone tried to kill her; he read them to get closer to her. Didn't matter, she left one day in 2002 and never looked back.

Half an hour into his shift, Ted got bored and put his book down. He ripped three pages off the movie trivia daily calendar the daytime security guard John left on their desk.

He paused on Friday, August 28.

MATCH THE REAL LIFE KILLER WITH THE ACTORS WHO PLAYED THEM

1. ZAC EFRON
2. JEREMY RENNER
3. GARY OLDMAN
4. CHARLIZE THERON

A. AILEEN WUORNOS
B. TED BUNDY
C. JEFFREY DAHMER
D. LEE HARVEY OSWALD

He scratched lines pairing 1 with B, 2 with C, and so on. Though he'd finished the quiz, he didn't rip the page off to reveal that day's challenge. He left Friday's page up because he wanted John to know he had some kind of brains in his head, even if it was for useless murder trivia.

Ted returned to his book. When he got to the middle, he found ten glossy pages of crime scene photos, including gory full body shots of human remains. He flipped past those as quickly as possible.

When the door behind him opened, he was too engrossed in his book to notice the squeak. He didn't hear the soft footsteps or sense the figure creeping slowly behind him. It wasn't until he felt a tap on his shoulder that he realized he wasn't alone.

He gasped in surprise and twisted around in his chair. He saw a figure in a dark hoodie, a pair of hands, big dark sunglasses over its eyes. He heard the person blow him a kiss, and inhaled a big breath to yell at them.

The powder went straight into his lungs.

He was out cold, slumped over his desk before he even knew what hit him.

CHAPTER 6

Where are we eating?

RIVER

I don't care as long as they have tasty desserts. I want to go into a sugar coma.

GRACIE

My mom has diabetes.

RIVER

Oh, whatever. Why can't we go to the Crave Inn? 25 kinds of pie...

BLYTHE

No. We're going there tomorrow. Variety is the spice.

CLAIRE

If you want spice, the Kluckin Chicken has it.

JAMES

I nearly burned my face off at that place. It was awesome.

BLYTHE

Heartburn. Plus, they serve their food in styrofoam containers. I'll get shit about climate change if I post from there.

GRACIE

Styrofoam is gross. They wouldn't be wrong…

RIVER

Aren't we the wet blanket today, Gracie.

GRACIE

STFU, River.

LOLLY

Indian food? There's a new place called Kurrypinch open over on Genesee.

MILA

Cute name!

JAMES

No way. First, let's ask ourselves if we think a place in Belldam will have good Indian. Second…does anyone really wanna smell Violet's ass all night?

VIOLET

I'm going to murder you, James.

JAMES

Not if I murder you first!

BLYTHE

I'm a no on Indian too. Idk if I can craft a post about Indian food without sounding racist.

CLAIRE

wtf

JAMES

Have you tried…not saying something racist?

BLYTHE

I'm not a racist! I just don't know if there are things out there that might be offensive to Indian people, and I don't wanna mess with it.

JAMES

Have you tried…not posting every meal on social media?

BLYTHE

It's easy content.

JAMES

Fine. What about burgers? Straight up, I'm okay with Whataburger.

BLYTHE

Noooooooooooooo! It needs to be unique!

CLAIRE

Seafood?

BLYTHE

Posted the catfish dinner from the Monument Inn on Wednesday.

MILA

How about at Sweet Orange?

BLYTHE

I did a vegan challenge last month. Ate at Sweet Orange six times. Don't y'all watch my videos?

CLAIRE

No. Never watch your videos. How about Duvall's?

BLYTHE

Maybe…

JAMES

No! Everything there tastes like brown gravy, even the banana split.

> **CLAIRE**
> JFC James. We almost had her.

> **VIOLET**
> Blythe, what do you suggest?

> **BLYTHE**
> I'm open to anything.

J ames turned in her seat to face me and lowered her window. She mimed throwing her phone from the car. I laughed and kicked the back of her seat.

"I'm going to strangle Blythe," she said. "You're prepared, right?"

I sighed. "Yeah."

"Why?" Heather asked.

"Group text," James said. "We're all on it. Everyone except Blythe is making suggestions. Blythe is shooting them down."

"She didn't shoot down Duvall's," I said.

"I'm not wrong about the gravy thing. You said yourself that their chopped chicken salad smelled like pot roast!"

"Why don't you go to the Jinkx Room?" Heather suggested. "Blythe loves it, they have a huge menu, and she hasn't gone in months."

"How do you know?" I asked.

"I follow her on social media."

"Of course you do," James said, shaking her head.

I fired off a text to the group.

> **VIOLET**
> What about the Jinkx Room?

> **BLYTHE**
> I LOVE the Jinkx Room!

I kicked James' seat.

"See?" I said. "Problem solved."

Minutes after we got back to James' house, Blythe's white Tesla X silently pulled into her driveway. She leapt from the car and threw her arms around Heather.

"Mrs. Parker, I haven't seen you in *forever!*"

"Please God, call me Heather, sweetie. Mrs. Parker makes me feel older than my daughter's sick burns."

James screamed. "I'm going to go on a Goddamn killing spree. I'm going to murder you and anyone else who heard you say that!"

Heather smirked.

"How have you been, Blythe?" she asked.

"Swamped. I have no idea how I'm going to keep up once school starts. I'm filming three times a week, and I already have a full schedule of meetings in LA and New York for fall break."

Heather gave a tight lipped smile. "I'm sure you can handle it. You always do."

"I know, right?" Blythe said, beaming.

In private, Heather made it clear she didn't like Blythe's online fame. She didn't find it healthy for a kid to be a "brand."

Blythe once offered to help James make some coding tutorials to upload to YouTube. She even offered to appear in them and promote them. Heather flipped out.

"You aren't going to put yourself out there in that way," she'd said. "You're a child. I don't want gross old men watching videos of you."

"They're tutorials for girls like me," said James. "Not old men."

"That's what you believe, and I'd love it to be true. It's not reality, though. You don't know who is watching you, or why. You want to do this after you move out, fine. You'll be an adult.

Until then, only people you know in real life get to follow your social media, and I get to monitor it how I see fit."

James smacked their kitchen counter. "Just because you grew up scared to meet people online doesn't mean that's how life is now."

Heather sighed and shook her head. "You're a very, very smart girl, James, but you don't have any idea what the real world is like. Even if pervs aren't watching you, it's not healthy. That girl doesn't have a plan. She's lost."

James punched a couch cushion. "She bought a hundred thousand dollar car and a beach house in Hawaii!" she squealed.

"It's not about money. I don't expect you to understand. My answer is no, discussion over."

Ever since then, when anyone mentioned Blythe, Heather looked sort of sad. Whether it was for Blythe or James, I couldn't tell.

Blythe hit a button, and her car's falcon-wing doors rose into the air. James slid into the second row. I sat shotgun. Heather waved and told us to be careful. James rolled down her window.

"In case I die, I love you, Mama! See you tomorrow morning!"

"Love you too, baby!" Heather yelled back. "See you if I don't die!"

Morbid goodbyes were a Parker family tradition. Their family always said they loved each other when they said goodbye in case something bad happened. Heather insisted. "You might not get another chance," she said.

James thought it was corny. I thought it was sweet.

More and more, we all questioned why we were still friends with Blythe.

We hadn't hung out in person in a while, not since the weekend after July 4th, when she had a pool party and invited about five hundred people. She asked Mila and me to come by early. James drove us.

Blythe had the full run of the second floor. She had three bedrooms, a bathroom, and a big living space where she set up a mini movie theater.

One of the bedrooms was, of course, where she slept. She also had a beauty room with packed clothes racks and floor to ceiling built-in cabinets for her massive makeup collection. It was roughly half the size of a Sephora, and overflowing with all the free junk beauty brands sent her.

The third bedroom was her filming room. Wallpaper from Anthropologie lined three walls – black and white doodled strawberries and peaches on soft mint green. The fourth wall was plain white and cluttered with industrial shelves and hooks to organize her filming equipment. Blythe hired an interior designer to accessorize the room, with a vanity to display her most recent sponsored products and a stunning hand-carved antique mirror. A vintage cinema lightbox sat on a bookshelf next to the vanity. Blythe changed the message on the lightbox for each video, usually to some weird sentence or quote to make people laugh. Previous quotes included: "How self-aware can a woman be with a parrot on her shoulder?" and "Lasagna: I'm only in it for the noodle."

Blythe paid someone to set up a professional lighting rig in the center of the room, and several microphones hung from the ceiling, just out of frame from her camera. Also out of frame were egg carton foam strips glued to the walls to absorb sound.

When Mila, James, and I arrived for the pool party, Blythe's mother Gwen drunkenly ushered us upstairs, where we found Blythe beating her face in her beauty room.

"Ahhhh!" she screamed. "I need so much help! I don't know what to wear!"

She pointed to a pile of bikinis on the floor.

"Why do you own so many plain red bikinis?" Mila asked.

"They're all different. Why? Should I do another color? Maybe a pattern?"

"Why are you wearing so much makeup when you'll be in the water later?" I asked. Blythe ignored me.

Mila shrugged. "Does it matter? It's kids from school. No one from Pritchett is gonna care."

"Yeah, but I need pictures. I'll probably throw up a couple video stories too."

I fished through the pile, unable to tell which pieces matched.

"I have a blue, pink, and purple tie-dye one," Blythe said. "Better?"

"Yes," James said. "Especially if you put it on your body right now, and we don't have to play dress up anymore."

Blythe gave James a once over. "Are you wearing a swimsuit under your stupid army jacket?"

James slipped off her jacket to show a simple black one-piece. Blythe picked up James' jacket and examined the pins and patches. My eyes watered when she breathed; the smell of vodka on her breath could've made her wallpaper peel.

"Oh my God!" Blythe screeched. "The 1970s Astros patch I got you for secret Santa!"

James nodded. "Yup. And the Game Boy Advance pin you got me for my birthday is next to it."

Blythe folded the jacket and placed it on a chair.

"I'm sorry I insulted your dad's jacket," Blythe said.

"It's fine," said James.

Blythe dug into a drawer and threw even more red swimsuits over her shoulder onto the pile. Finally, at the bottom, she found the tie-dye. She ran behind a curtain hanging in the corner to change. When she finished, she flung the curtain back, threw her arms above her head, and sang, "Tah dah!"

Mila gasped. "Blythe, your body looks incredible!"

"Dude, thank you," said Blythe. "So many eggs, so much chicken, so much spinach, so many squats."

"Sounds like work," said James.

"Too much work," I said. "I'll stick to being skinny fat."

Blythe ignored us. She found a white kimono and put it on over the bikini, then she ran to her filming room, returning with a camera and some white poster board.

"Let's go out on the balcony and take some pics," she said, handing the camera to me, and the poster board to James.

"What is this?" James asked.

"A fill card," said Blythe. "For lighting. We probably won't need it if the natural light is good. Better to bring it and not need it."

James made a stank face, which Blythe also ignored.

"Mila, Violet, do you want to be in the pictures?"

Mila said sure. I turned her down because I'd already slathered myself in greasy sunscreen.

We followed Blythe onto her balcony, and I photographed Blythe and Mila while James stood off to the side. Blythe declared the natural lighting good and threw the fill card to the side, leaving James with no task.

If life was a drinking game, and we took a shot each time James rolled her eyes during the shoot, we'd all have alcohol poisoning.

Since life wasn't a drinking game, none of us were taking any shots...except for Blythe. She had tossed a towel on the ground, and when she and Mila adjusted their poses, Blythe would kneel and take a big swig from a star-shaped flask hidden in the towel. By the time we finished, a fresh sunburn had seared my scalp, and James' swimsuit had a big wet spot on the front where she'd drenched it with sweat.

"I'm not going to follow this bitch around all day playing camera crew," James whispered into my ear.

"No one asked us to," I said.

"Not. Yet." Her words came out short and sharp.

James edged toward the door, and the party hadn't even started yet. We'd all been in this situation with Blythe before. I checked the time on my phone and decided we'd be leaving early. I'd rather hang out in a half-full kiddie pool in my backyard than babysit Blythe's drunk ass while James bitched all day.

Her bitching stopped as soon as the guests came.

Nolan Flynn, a guy James had a painful crush on, arrived and gave James a new focal point. When he walked in, she disappeared. I found her hiding in the kitchen behind a pantry door.

"I've never been so embarrassed in my life," she whispered.

"What did you do?" I asked.

"Nothing yet, I just don't want Nolan to be aware of my existence."

On cue, Blythe poured herself into the room, Nolan on her arm. She led him to us, her eyes locked on James.

"James built my website for me this summer," Blythe whispered to Nolan.

His face lit up. "You did?" he asked James.

James stared at him blankly, saying nothing. We all leaned in, waiting for her to answer.

Finally, she breathed a soft, "Yes."

"You founded the coding club at school, right?" Nolan asked.

James nodded.

"Can anyone join?" he asked.

James blinked.

I wanted to shove my arm up her butt and turn her into a puppet and answer his incredibly basic questions for her. Blythe sensed my incoming intervention and pulled me away. James watched us leave, panic in her eyes.

"I invited him for her," she told me. "I saw her quietly freak out around him at Hannah Tyson's graduation party last May, and I knew. His dad owns the company that does our landscaping. Nolan works for him in the summer. He's mowed my lawn for months, and when I see him, I tell him about my amazing friend James.

"She's going to kill you," I said.

"She's going to make me a bridesmaid," Blythe slurred, her eyes pointing in two different directions.

"How much have you had to drink?" I asked.

"Not enough," she laughed. She pulled me close and made me smile for a selfie. She examined the photo and tapped the screen. "Your scalp is blood red. Let's go find you a cute hat before you burst into flames."

That day was a perfect illustration of who Blythe had become. Half the time, she acted like a drunken social media guru, concerned only with her next YouTube video or Tweet.

Other times the old Blythe would shine through, the girl we loved before she became internet famous. Silly and outgoing, ready to cut off her arm for the people she loved. Her sweet side translated into her content, which made everyone, even strangers, want to be her best friend.

If you could get past the photoshoots, that is.

To my surprise, photoshoots weren't going to be an issue at the Senior Scavenge.

"I'm confiscating phones tonight," Blythe announced when we reached our table at the restaurant. The hostess placed lemon water next to our plates. Blythe took a dramatic sip. "I'll be locking them in my glove compartment."

"Including your phone?" asked Gracie.

Blythe nodded.

Mila pretended to fall off her chair. "I'm sorry, did Blythe Lennon, makeup guru, comedienne, influencer, internet-goddess-queen say she's leaving her phone in the car?"

Blythe dipped her fingers in her water and flicked them at Mila. "Bitch, don't. I'm capable of having fun without documenting it. I need to get a good chick pic first. I have a great joke about chicken breast I want to use for the caption."

"That's our girl!" laughed James.

I craved cheese fries, so I didn't even bother to take a menu.

While the others decided their orders, I scanned the room. It appeared that all the parents in Belldam chose to bring their kids that night to screech and torture strangers. One of the waitresses seemed particularly stressed. Little identical twin boys had crawled under their table as she tried to take their order. They each had a red balloon and growled like monsters.

"Please stop playing Pennywise and sit in your seats," begged their mother. Mom looked like she wanted to sink into the floor. Dad looked like he wanted to storm out and leave them. The waitress looked like she wanted to cry. She twisted her head to the side, rubbing her temples.

I gasped when I recognized her.

"Isn't that Emma Tucker?" I whispered to the group. "Y'all, do not turn around."

Mila, unable to resist, turned her front-facing camera on and lifted it to sneak a covert peek.

"It totally is," she said.

Blythe's eyes widened. "Didn't she go to Harvard last year?"

"Yeah," said James. "I got way too drunk at her going away party. Violet had to drive me home."

"If it was bad enough to let Violet drive, you must've been *obliterated*," Blythe said.

I kicked Blythe under the table. James grinned.

Then, as if she could sense us watching, Emma's head turned in our direction. She closed her eyes for a second, took a breath, and walked over.

"Hey, guys! Long time no see!" she said, flashing a strained smile.

Blythe jumped up and gave Emma a tight hug. "What are you doing in town?" she asked.

"Working to save money for when I go back to school," Emma said, her eyes fixed on the salt and pepper shakers.

"You're at Harvard, right?" asked James.

"Mmmhmm. It's great."

"When do you go back?" I asked. It surprised me to see her in Belldam so late in the summer. Most college kids were back in their dorms by August.

"A week or so," Emma said. "Hey, I'm so sorry. We're super busy tonight. What can I get you guys?"

We sat in awkward silence while Emma stood frozen with her pad and paper. James shot me a look. Emma's story didn't add up, and we both knew it.

"I'll go first," said Mila. "Can I please have the chicken sandwich with waffle fries and instead of a side salad a fruit cup? And a lemonade, please."

"You got it," said Emma, scribbling on her pad.

Mila gave her a little salute and switched her attention to her phone.

"Cheese fries and a lemon bar please," I said. Emma nodded.

"What's the tortilla thing with the parmesan garlic crust?" asked James.

Emma craned her neck to check James' menu. She pointed her pen at an item. "Vampire quesadilla?"

James smiled. "I'd like the quesadilla and a Shirley Temple."

"Turkey chili and another water, please," said Claire.

"Chili in August?" River asked, gagging.

"Protein," said Claire.

River ordered grilled cheese sandwiches and cherry Cokes for both herself and Gracie.

Lolly got a big salad and a Neapolitan milkshake.

Then all heads turned to Blythe.

"Okay, this might be strange, bear with me. I want the fried chicken breast, but I want the crunchiest, brownest, most unappetizing fried chicken you have. If you can, have the cook leave all the grease on it when it comes out of the fryer. I'd like french fries, but I'd like them mushy and covered in black pepper. I'd also like creamed corn. Is that okay? Oh, and a slice of zebra cheesecake. If possible, can it come out at the same time? Please?"

Emma blinked. "Um, I'll see what I can do. Does anyone want anything else?"

We told her we were good. Emma left to explain to the kitchen that she had a lunatic customer demanding placation.

"Are you for real?" asked James.

"What?" Blythe asked. "I'm going to claim it came from a snooty French bistro. It's funny." She shrugged and tucked her menu back into the holder. "I'm going to eat all the food, leave a huge tip, and I'm not saying the restaurant's real name."

I wondered whether or not a big tip made it worth the headache.

"Guys, forget about Blythe's gross-ass food," Mila said. "Emma acted all weird, so I texted Jaden Peters."

James gulped some water. "Her ex?" she asked.

"Yeah. He said Harvard kicked Emma out. She stopped going to classes after February."

"How can you get into Harvard and stop going to class?" I asked, stunned. If I managed to get into DSU, I'd do anything I could to stay.

"He said she had a nervous breakdown or something. The stress got to her. She's taking a year off, and she's applying to local schools after."

"This is why I'm deferring for a year while Gracie and I write the book," said River. "Why go through all that? Plus nowadays a degree doesn't mean much. How many people do we know who got their Bachelor's and are now stuck working retail?"

"Eva, this girl my mom works with, got her Masters in psychology. She's front desk manager at the Belldam Tower," I said. "She makes 35k, and she's got like a hundred thousand in student loans."

"See?" said River. "You can't tell me Eva needs a degree for her job. She wouldn't have all the debt either."

"A degree was a requirement for the job," I said.

"Isn't her job to check people into the hotel and be nice to them?" asked James.

"I think it's more than that," I said. "But it's definitely not something you need a Masters for. Anyone polite with organizational skills and a couple years at the desk could do her job."

Blythe sighed. "It's all so depressing."

"Says the self-made multi-millionaire," James joked.

"Money comes and goes," said Blythe.

James' eyes bulged. *"Says the self-made multi-millionaire,"* she repeated.

Blythe suddenly became extremely interested in her fork. "Money isn't everything," she whispered. "It doesn't guarantee a better future. Maybe you're all the lucky ones, going off to school, writing books, doing something real, something important. Maybe I'm jealous of y'all."

James opened her mouth to repeat herself a third time. I pinched her leg before she could speak.

No one wanted to listen to James yell at Blythe about college degrees. However, Blythe had a point. You shouldn't need a degree to work most jobs.

James, with her future set at A&M, couldn't see the other side. Her personal experience clouded her vision, and honestly, it bugged me a little. She tried her best to not mention college around me, but it was inescapable; even on the night of the Scavenge, she was wearing an Aggie t-shirt with her denim shorts and army jacket. Sometimes she'd drone on about her plans and how much her dad loved going there, which felt like a weird double brag. I couldn't help but think, "Oh, you're going to school without me, and you've got a dad. Big woo."

Lolly's phone chimed. I could see her mom's face fill the screen. She excused herself and ran outside to answer the call.

"Let's change the subject," I said. "Does everyone have their invites? Have we all solved our riddles?"

"Ours are in the car," said Gracie, her head nodding toward River.

"Mine too," said Claire. "It's in my backpack."

We dug through our bags. Mila cleared the table, and we arranged them in a row. James' dunk tank and my Ferris wheel lay side by side with a creepy palm reader robot puppet thing and a plaster clown head with a gaping mouth.

I picked up Mila's card, the clown, and flipped it over. Her poem read:

> HERE IN TEXAS, WE LIKE GUNS
> SHOOTING EVIL CLOWNS IS SO MUCH FUN.
> NO BULLETS FOR THIS GUY, ONLY A SQUIRT
> LOOK UNDER HIS CHIN, BUT ABOVE THE DIRT.

"What's under the clown's chin?" I asked.

Mila took her card from me and put it back in her purse. "You squirt water into his mouth, and it fills a balloon stuck under his chin. I think I need to get a balloon."

"Makes sense," said James.

"I have to get one of those generic palm reading cards from the mannequin," said Blythe. She picked up her card and read her poem aloud. "Madame Lavona can't turn her head, she's got those blank eyes, like the walking dead. She might be creepy, held together with twine. Still, she can answer, how long's your lifeline?"

"Kinda dark," said James. "Awesome."

"Delilah has a dark sense of humor," Blythe said, shivering. "She knows how much I can't stand the thing. The song it plays, how the whole body juts back and forth, and the way the eyes roll back in her head while the card prints. Ugh."

Emma swung past the table and silently refilled our water glasses. Did she know we knew she'd left Harvard? A twinge of guilt made me blush. I shouldn't have gossiped about her.

Finally, a busboy brought our food. Blythe made us hold our plates in our laps while she arranged her chicken, fries, and corn in the least appetizing way possible. James and I exchanged a glance. Her thoughts came in loud and clear.

Why are we playing along with this circus?

Lolly came back as Blythe was photographing her dessert. She found her food in her chair and frowned.

"Two seconds," Blythe told her, raising two fingers. "We can all split the cheesecake."

"Eight people eating a tiny sliver," said Mila, rolling her eyes. "Y'all can have it. I'm getting a sundae."

CHAPTER 7

Blythe paid the check while I went to pee, and everyone else went outside. When I finished in the bathroom, I passed Emma cleaning our table. The other patrons had cleared out; she was alone in her section of the dining room. After a brief internal argument, I decided to talk to her.

"Hey, Emma," I said.

She placed her tray on the table. "Violet. Hey." Her voice was flat, her skin mottled grey, and half circles darkened under her eyes.

I immediately regretted saying hello. If I'd been smart, I'd have mumbled something about how nice it was to see her, and I'd have said goodbye.

Since I was a dumbass, I chose to rip out her throat and spew word vomit into the wound.

"I know you left Harvard," I said, my voice high and thin. I smiled, my worst nervous tic.

Emma's shoulders slumped. "Wow. Cool. A little girl who has never left her mommy is about to mock me. Awesome. I'll give you credit, at least you have the guts to do it to my face. Nobody can shut up behind my back."

A voice inside my head screamed, *"Run!"*

"Emma," I said. "Oh God, I didn't mean it that way. I meant it's awful. I've been going through something, and I thought you might understand, and maybe I understand you."

"I've got tables to clean before I can leave this hellhole, Violet. Can you please skip to the part where you explain what you're talking about?"

"Everybody's gotten accepted into college. I haven't. I only applied to my dream school, so I'm petrified."

Emma's pressed her lips into a straight line. She picked up a fork and threw it on her tray. Then she slammed some glasses on the table. She grabbed a steak knife, got a glint in her eye, and stared right into my soul.

"I wanted to go to Harvard more than anything in my life," Emma said. She stepped forward and held the knife under my chin. "My mom didn't go to college, and she was always ashamed. I wanted to make her proud. I didn't want to go to just any college. I wanted to go to *the* college. I worked my ass off my entire life to get there. And unlike *you*, I did. Early admission even. No one had ever cried as hard as my mom did when I told her. Pure pride."

She gently pressed the knife into my jugular. Nervous laughter jittered inside my body, but I swallowed it before it could burst through.

"It's sharp," I whispered.

Emma ignored me and continued. "I walked around all cocky Senior year bragging about Harvard, and I mentioned it in my speech at graduation. The entire town of Belldam knew. Then I got to Harvard. All the students worked as hard as I did, many harder—literal geniuses around every corner. Most of them came from major money. Intimidation as far as the eye can see. I stopped sleeping to study, and I started having anxiety attacks. I couldn't handle leaving my bed to go to class. I was so freaked out I'd fail them. Turns out, if you don't go to class, you fail by default. I hid in my dorm room until someone from the school came and dragged me out."

"That's awful," I said. I took a step back.

Emma took a step forward. She kept the knife at my throat.

"Now my mom can't even look me in the eye," she said. "I moved into the garage because I can't be around her, and I can't afford to move. Now I get to sweat my ass off waiting on people who know about Harvard, and who say stupid, hurtful shit to me about it. Like you, who thinks being rejected is the same as what I went through."

She narrowed her eyes and used the knife to scratch the soft flesh under my chin.

"I'm sorry," I said, my voice soft.

"You will be," she said, smiling. She snatched bills Blythe left as a tip and counted it. "One day, you'll see. You'll be sorry. Tell Blythe thanks, but $100 isn't enough to deal with her bullshit."

Emma folded the cash and put it in her pocket.

I whispered another apology.

She'd already walked away.

River and Gracie got in River's Honda and sped off.

I slid into the front seat of Blythe's Tesla. The others debated who would ride in which car.

"All y'all can fit in the X," Blythe insisted.

"I don't want to leave my car here overnight," Mila said.

"It's open 24 hours and has a bright parking lot," Blythe countered. "It's probably safer to leave it here than in the woods by the carnival."

Mila stood firm. She asked if anyone wanted to ride with her. James leapt at the offer.

"Seriously, dude?" asked Blythe. "Fine. If people don't want to ride with me, I'm not going to hold them hostage. Lolly, Claire, you can ride with Mila. Violet and I will go it alone."

"You don't have to get huffy," said Claire.

Blythe climbed into the driver's seat, slammed the door, and lowered her window.

"I'm not being huffy," she said. "I want some alone time with my buddy V."

She threw the car in reverse and shot out of her spot, nearly mowing Lolly down. Before we left the lot, I turned back to check on the others. Claire and James were laughing while Mila comforted a shaken Lolly.

"Geez, you didn't have to murder Lolly just because James wanted to ride with Mila."

"Is she mad at me?" Blythe asked.

"Who?"

"Who? James. Duh."

"No," I said. "I mean, James hasn't said anything to me."

"She's pissed I took the photos at dinner."

I ignored her and ran my fingers along the white leather seat.

"How do you not get the inside of this car filthy?" I asked. "White seats, white steering wheel, white everything. If it were mine, it would be brown by now."

"I don't have a choice."

"Didn't you choose white? Isn't it custom?"

"Not the car. The photos. I do three posts a day. Meal pics are easy, and they always get tons of likes. Selfies get more, but I can't only post pictures of myself. If it's me in my house or whatever, no one cares. With school starting, I can't leave Belldam as much, and I've exhausted all my options around here."

I didn't know what to say. My life was a first world problem compared to whatever the hell Emma was going through.

"You gotta do what you gotta do," I finally said.

"This is why I love you, Violet. You get it. Speaking of getting it, have you heard from DSU?"

"No," I groaned. "And I don't want to talk about it. I'm not getting in. I'm so far from being accepted that DSU isn't going to send me a rejection."

"You could always be my intern. We could go to Europe!"

I smiled. It was an offer most people couldn't refuse. For me, carrying Blythe's bags around the world sounded like hell, like my dream being flushed down the toilet.

"While a trip to Europe would be awesome," I said. "I'm still devastated."

"Imagine being devastated in Paris."

She spoke in the same tone as a character on a children's show trying to convince preschoolers to eat their vegetables. She looked at me, eyebrows raised, and almost swerved into an oncoming bus.

"Whoa," I said. "No one is going to Paris if we're dead."

Blythe turned her attention back to the road.

"Sorry I almost killed us."

"Speaking of killing people," I said. "Emma tried to slit my throat."

"What?" Blythe laughed. "When?"

"On my way out. I stopped to say goodbye. I mentioned Harvard."

"Wow. You're an asshole."

"I completely lost my mind!" I screeched. "I wanted to commiserate!"

"Yeah…"

"I wish she'd have done it. I'd rather be dead than wait tables at Jinkx next to her."

Blythe rolled to a stop at a red light. The street was empty, save for us and a black cat strutting across the intersection.

"Well, I don't know about you, but I plan to live forever, even if I have to be a waitress," she said. She paused, then gasped. "Hey, let's play the traffic light game!"

We created the traffic light game one night not long after Blythe got her license. Her mother banned her from leaving Belldam without an adult, and she watched Blythe's GPS like a hawk. When we got bored and had no place to go, we would drive around town aimlessly until the battery needed recharging.

One night, Blythe's phone buzzed in her purse. She asked me to check if the text was from her mom.

CLIFF H

When RU back in LA?

"Who is Cliff H?" I asked.

"Did he text?"

"Yeah."

Blythe sighed. "Cliff Horne."

I dropped the phone. "The guy from the *Xylophone Man* reboot?" I gasped.

"Yeah…" Blythe said. I waited for her to explain. Instead, she turned up the radio and sang along with Andrew McMahon. I leaned forward to catch her eye. She ignored me.

I slapped the screen and turned the music off.

"What?" she asked. "I was getting into the song!"

"Why is there a 25 year old actor texting you?"

"When I was in LA doing press for my Sizzle Seltzer sponsorship, my agent took me to dinner. Cliff was one of the other guests. We bonded over our love for the *Terminator* movies, and he bought me my first Old Fashioned."

"He got you drunk?"

She snorted. "I was already drunk when he met me."

Suddenly I felt small, like a child needing her mom. I knew Blythe liked to party at home with boys from Belldam. I had no idea she went to bars with grown men.

"Does he know how old you are?" I asked.

"I don't care."

Blythe turned the music back on and shimmied in her seat.

"Are you going to text him back?" I asked.

"If the next light is green, I tell him I'll hook up with him in LA. Red, I say no."

When we got to the light, it was red.

"Go ahead," she said. "Shoot Cliffy Boy down."

"What do I say?"

"Whatever your sweet lil heart desires."

I bit my lip and tried to think like Blythe.

Aren't I a little mature for you?

I showed the text to Blythe. She approved. Seconds later, Cliff responded that he was joking anyway, she was too fat for him, and her accent made her sound like a hick. I'd have been devastated if someone said those things to me, Blythe laughed.

Less than a week later, the cops arrested Cliff for having sex with a fourteen year old girl. Blythe had dodged one big ass bullet thanks to the red light.

Ever since that night, when we had a dilemma, we asked the traffic lights for an answer.

"Should Violet come to Europe with me after graduation?" she asked the next light. It flipped from green to yellow as we reached the intersection "Damn. We'll see what the next one says."

She continued driving. As we approached the next light, Blythe asked, "Is Violet going to agree to come with me to Europe?"

The second light also turned yellow.

"One more time," she said, accelerating the car. "Will Violet be coming with me to Europe after graduation?"

She turned left onto Cedar Bayou Road. Ahead, all the shops were closed, all the porch lights were out, all the street lights were dark, and all the traffic lights for miles flashed red.

Blythe pressed the brake, and we sat frozen in the street, staring out at the sea of lights screaming, "No!"

"What the hell does this mean?" I asked.

A chilly breeze blew through the cabin. Blythe raised her window. She gripped the wheel, her breathing slow and dry.

"Maybe it means no one is going to Europe," she whispered. "The lights never lie."

CHAPTER 8

We didn't want anyone to see our cars in the lot, so we parked in the woods.

Claire, ever the team captain, appointed herself our leader.

"We should break into pairs," she said. "I've got a map on my phone. We'll split up based on which landmarks are in closest proximity."

"Boooooo," said Mila. "I want to get this done so we can get out of here. Let's go alone and meet at the entrance after."

"No," said James. "We need to get it done so we can explore the creepy abandoned carnival."

"What a stupid idea," said Lolly. "We could get caught. We could get arrested. I want to go to college next year, not prison."

"Speaking of prison," Gracie said, her eyes sliding in River's direction. "Whatcha got in your pocket, Miss Ellis?"

River grinned, showing the slight gap between her front teeth. She'd had braces in middle school, then refused to wear her retainer, so they shifted apart. Her parents were pissed. I thought it gave her character.

She reached into her leather crossbody bag and produced a Ziploc filled with squishy orange circus peanut candy.

"Are we locking people up for sugar abuse now?" asked Claire. "How do those relate to prison?

"My cousin from Denver gave these to me when he visited in June. These babies each have twenty milligrams of THC in them. I figured they'd make tonight a little more fun."

We looked around to gauge the other's reactions.

Finally, James asked, "Isn't twenty a lot?"

"For me, no," said River. "For you, probably. Luckily they're easy to tear in half."

"No effing way," said Lolly. "Never mind getting caught, how are we going to get home?"

"My brother said he'd drive us," River said. "He's got his pickup. We can ride in the back."

I'd been in the back of Reed Ellis' truck before. There was a 1970s exploitation film showing at a drive-in theater in Austin. River asked if a few of us wanted to go, and I said yes. I found myself laying in the back, one hand grasping a spare tire, the other gripping James' leg, as the old Chevy barreled down the highway at 110 miles an hour.

I pictured the eight of us, high off our asses, riding in the back of Reed's truck through Belldam. It was easy to imagine a situation where someone, probably Mila, jumped, and tried to fly. I pictured her little body hurtling through the air into the branches of the ugly tree that grew up through the pavement in the center of Belldam Boulevard.

I'd feel safer letting a rabid monkey drive us home.

"Lolly has a point," I said. "Do y'all really want to leave your cars here in the woods?"

"Thank you, Violet," Lolly said. I nodded in solidarity.

Lolly was the ultimate goody two shoes. Awake at six, in bed by ten. She was the only teenager I'd ever met who watched her fiber intake. The girl had perfect attendance since Kindergarten. Once she got a 94 on an algebra quiz, and ugly cried. Despite her "terrible" grades - insert James style eye roll here - there was no question she would be valedictorian.

She served as the voice of reason in precarious situations, and it was a good thing we had her. Who else would keep James from hacking into teacher's emails, or tell Blythe it was a bad idea to post pictures of herself drinking a margarita online? Lolly was the best type of mom friend, always saving us from ourselves.

"Laaaaaame," River whined.

James raised her hand. "I'll do it. Gimme." She held out a hand. River beamed and pressed a peanut into her palm. As she opened her mouth to warn James to take it slow, James shoved the whole thing in her mouth.

"Mmmm," said James. "It doesn't taste like weed, but it sure tastes like food dye."

"I'm not going to be the one cradling you, telling you you're fine," Lolly warned James. "If you flip and demand to go to the ER, I won't be the one to talk you down."

James grinned. "Yes, you will because you love me."

Lolly scowled. "Yeah, yeah."

Gracie took two, ate one and a half, and put the rest in her pocket. Mila told her she would get lint all over it. Gracie pointed out that by the time she was ready to eat it, she'd be so stoned she wouldn't care about lint.

Claire ate five peanuts. Lolly asked what would happen if her coach drug tested her.

"Weirdly she doesn't drug test. The district doesn't require it, and secretly she's scared to find out someone is on steroids."

"There we go," said River. "Mila wants one, but she's not going to ask."

River handed Mila a peanut, which she nibbled daintily. "A lady doesn't ask for illegal substances," She said. "A lady waits to be invited."

"What does that even mean?" I asked.

"I have no idea," said Mila.

"I'll take three," Blythe said, ignoring us. She nodded at

River. "Seth Rogen over here gave me a 10mg gummy bear a few weeks ago. Didn't feel a thing."

River did a quick headcount. "Violet and Lolly, you're the hold outs."

Lolly grabbed my arm, squeezing the skin until I yelped.

"I need to talk to you alone," she said.

She led me around behind the cars, away from the other girls.

"What's wrong?" I asked.

"Please tell me you're not doing this."

I knew she wanted me to stay sober because it would take the pressure off her. It's easier to say no when you have a buddy. Usually, I'd have told her, "Yes, I'll stay sober with you, no problem." But that night, I needed to shut off my brain.

"It might be fun," I said. "I'll eat a little more than half, and you can have the rest."

Lolly's bottom lip quivered. "I've never done drugs."

This news wasn't a surprise.

"Yes, you have," I said. "When you got your wisdom teeth out. You took Vicodin and sang Selena Gomez to me for an hour. Off-key, I might add."

"That's different."

"Drugs are drugs, so not really. Look, you don't have to if you don't want to."

"I know." She squinted at the trees and mumbled, "Except...I kinda want to."

I slapped my chest and staggered back in over exaggerated shock.

"Little Miss Lolly Bishop," I exclaimed. "What are you saying?"

"I've always been curious. It's a bad idea. Do you remember what happened when I ate a Jello shot at Gracie's July 4th Party in Galveston?"

"You mean when you fell down the stairs and cried because the Gulf doesn't have blue water?"

She nodded. "I want you to stop me," she said softly. "Do not let me eat weed candy."

I smiled. "Or maybe you'd rather I give you permission?"

Lolly stared back up at the trees. "Everyone thinks I'm the mom friend."

"You *are* the mom friend," I interrupted. "It's not a bad thing."

She continued. "Do you know how many times I've driven River home from a party because she's stoned out of her gourd? Or how even though I sprained my wrist falling down the stairs, I held back Gracie's hair when she went in on the Jello shots? Or covered for Mila because she wanted to spend the night with Tyler? Or counseled my crazy friend Violet when she has panic attacks about the future?"

"You're comparing my freakouts to Mila banging her boyfriend in his attic?"

"I want to have fun," Lolly moaned dramatically. "I'm a teenager too. Teenagers experiment."

"You sound like an out of touch adult in an anti-drug commercial."

Lolly gave me a little shove. "If you do it, I will. If you don't, I won't."

I considered my options. On the one hand, it would be hilarious to see Lolly high. On the other, she might not like it, and we'd have to find a way to help her chill out.

"Answer one question," I said. "What brought this on?"

She sighed. "My sister."

Lolly's sister Gina was like Lolly on steroids, roid rage, and all. She was a teacher's pet type, and judgmental as hell. She relished calling other people out. Gina's Senior year, a classmate threw a house party after the homecoming game. It was at a mansion in Blythe's neighborhood. All Pritchett students got an invite, even Gina. Her friends convinced her to go. "It's homecoming!" her friends said. "We're Seniors!" When they got there, Gina saw a keg, turned around, and walked to the main road. She made two phone calls: One call to her mother to take her home, the other to the cops. They came to the party and dragged anyone who couldn't run fast enough back to the station in a police van.

Everyone under the age of eighteen in Belldam loathed her after that.

"What about your sister?" I asked, feigning ignorance.

"She's just...such a bitch," Lolly said. "Remember when I kissed Oscar Pine?"

"How could I forget! It was the greatest scandal of all time."

"Gina called me a slut."

I wanted to laugh. "You didn't even use tongue!."

"Right? It was nothing. I don't want to be my sister. I don't want people to hate me, and honestly, sometimes I hear her voice coming from my mouth, and it makes me hate myself."

I took a deep breath. What Lolly needed now was her own mom friend.

"First of all, you are not your sister. Know why? Because you're there doing things like holding back hair and lying about sleepovers. You might not do questionable stuff yourself, but you also don't care if we do. There's a difference. You're a really good friend. You let people make mistakes, and then you help them recover."

"Thanks," she said softly.

"Second of all, if you want to eat a peanut, eat the damn peanut. It's weed, not heroin. You can't overdose on it; it won't kill you. It's safer than liquor, even. I've done it before. You'll feel weird and kinda loose, and it kinda makes you view things from a different perspective."

"How so?"

"Well, James and I ate some chocolate and watched *The Little Mermaid*. Before I thought it was gross, she left her ocean princess life for a guy. When we watched it high, I realized Ariel always wanted to be a human and live on land, long before she even met him. Eric was the catalyst that allowed her to take the leap."

"I never thought of it like that."

"You see my point. Edibles aren't something I want to do daily, but they're harmless fun every once in a while as long as you are with friends and aren't operating heavy machinery. If you want to try it, try it," I said. "Question. What's your item for the hunt?"

"A stuffed muscle man prize from the test your strength game."

"Okay. It will take a minute for the peanut to kick in. You run to the game and get the toy, I'll get my pass for the Ferris wheel, and we'll meet at the carousel and hang out. I've got you."

"You're doing it too, though, right?" Her big brown eyes were damp.

I laced my fingers in hers.

"Sure," I said, patting her hand. "When we're done, we'll go over to Blythe's house, lay by the pool, and gaze at the stars. There are so many out tonight."

Above us, through the trees, tiny twinkling lights dotted the sky. We stood in silence, gazing, while Lolly took a minute to digest her decision.

Finally, she exhaled and nodded. I put my arm around her shoulder and pulled her back to the others.

"River," I said. "Give me a peanut."

River's eyes widened. She held out the bag. I took one, ate two thirds, and handed the rest to Lolly, who threw it back and swallowed it without chewing.

Everyone else froze for a second, processed what they'd witnessed, and broke out into applause. Lolly's face turned pink.

Our celebration was cut short by a crash deep in the woods.

"What the hell?" whispered Blythe.

"Probably a deer," said Claire.

Blythe motioned in the direction of the sound. "Claire, go check it out."

"Why me?"

"Because you can deadlift an SUV."

"I can't deadlift an SUV!" Claire said. "Thank you so much for saying I could! I saw Brie Larson push a Jeep online, and I want to do it so bad."

Blythe gasped. She'd been lifting weights since February as part of a social media challenge. Claire was her coach; they got together four days a week to work out.

"You and me pushing Jeeps by Halloween?" Blythe stuck out a hand to seal the deal.

Before Claire could respond, the bushes shook. A man's shadowy figure burst from the leaves.

"What are you girls doing?" he asked. "You shouldn't be out this late!"

The bushes rustled again, and a big black dog bolted toward the man. As he stepped into the light, I recognized the shadowy figure was Mr. Luzon, a ninth-grade English teacher at Pritchett.

River cocked her head. "Mr. Luzon?"

"River?" he asked. He took a headcount. "Mila? *Lolly?*"

My skin crawled. Mr. Luzon had a reputation for being a creep. He liked to rub girl's shoulders during class and often offered to tutor the prettiest girls at his house.

"Hi, Mr. Luzon," said Lolly. She stepped forward, putting her body between him and the rest of us. "How are you?"

"Fine," he said. "Walking my dog, Bubbles. Little surprised to see you ladies out here."

"Well, we're doing the Senior Scavenge," Lolly said in the syrupy voice she always used with authority figures. "Incoming Senior girls do every year."

"Isn't the scavenger hunt supposed to be at the school?" he asked.

"This year, it's at the carnival," Lolly replied.

Mr. Luzon stroked Bubbles' head. Bubbles growled low and long. The ground vibrated beneath my feet.

"You get permission?" he asked.

Lolly smiled. "Of course. The girls who arranged it talked to security. We promised not to damage anything, and we aren't taking anything valuable. As long as we're out before sunrise, we're fine."

I was stunned. Lolly's lied so smoothly it sounded like *she* believed it.

But Bubbles didn't buy it. She barked and gnashed her teeth at Lolly.

Mr. Luzon grabbed Bubbles by the collar. Bubbles growled and pulled away. Mr. Luzon yanked her back with such force she yelped in pain. James stepped forward, as though she wanted to wrestle the dog from him. Bubbles didn't want the help. She snapped at James, missing her fingers by inches.

"Don't mess with my dog," Mr. Luzon yelled. "She's attack trained. She knows you don't belong here." He hunched over and put his face a little too close to Lolly's. My muscles tightened as I prepared to intervene. He raised a finger at me.

"There are wicked people in this town," he said. "People who like to hurt little girls. You should've kept this at the school. It's safe there."

Lolly didn't flinch. "It's safe here too. There's a guard on duty. We'll be less than an hour."

"A guard, eh?" Mr. Luzon chuckled. "Funny thing. I like to walk Bubbles around the parking lot. The night guard Ted and I are friendly. I stopped by the guard stand tonight to say hello. He wasn't there. When we finished our walk, I swung by again. No Ted. His car is missing. I don't think he's working tonight."

"I'm sure that's not true," said Lolly. "He probably ran to get dinner. He's letting us in at midnight. It's only 11:50 now. He'll probably drive up as we reach the gate."

Mr. Luzon considered her words. Bubbles pulled at the collar and snapped at James again. Foamy spit formed at the corners of her mouth and flew through the air.

"You should probably worry less about our scavenger hunt and more about your dog's rabies," James said.

"My dog ain't got rabies. She's anxious because she wants you away from her territory."

"Ain't got rabies," Lolly chuckled. "Impressive language for an English teacher."

Mr. Luzon turned red. He sputtered a nonsensical reply and poked her in the chest with his index finger. I took her by the shoulders and moved her away.

"You just put your hands on a teenage girl," I said. I stared into his eyes, willing myself not to blink. "Didn't you get in trouble for that a few years ago? Didn't you tell a Freshman she needed to button her top button and try to do it for her?"

His hand twitched like he might release his hound on me.

"What is your point, Miss Warren?" he asked.

"We have permission to go into the carnival," I said. "You don't have permission to touch us. If you think we won't tell the entire town you're a perv, you're sadly mistaken."

"I barely touched her!" he yelped.

"Doesn't matter," I said. "Look around. Who is standing before you? The future valedictorian. The queen of the athletics department. A legit celebrity. We're at the top of the Pritchett High food chain. You're a gross old man with years of nasty rumors following you around. Are they going to believe your scummy ass or eight sweet little girls?"

Someone behind me gasped. I couldn't tell who.

Mr. Luzon's face was purple and sweaty. "Fine," he said. "Have it your way. If you want to wander off to your deaths, be my guest."

"Is that a threat?" I asked.

"Psh. As if I'd waste my time threatening you little bitches."

He yanked Bubbles again, this time back toward the bushes.

When he was out of sight, we all started talking at once.

"Did he call us bitches?" I asked.

"Did you two seriously talk to him like that?" asked Mila.

"What if he calls the cops?" asked Blythe. "I mean, my dad can get us out of it if he answers my call."

"Is there actually a guard?" asked Gracie.

"Is anyone else high?" asked Lolly.

Blythe held out a zippered leather clutch with HELLO embossed on the front and GOODBYE embossed on the back. She demanded our phones. There were grumbles, but she insisted.

"If I have to leave my phone in the car, y'all do too," she told us.

One by one, we dropped our phones in the bag. Blythe kept hers in her hand. When the bag was full, she put it on the ground and told us to squeeze together for one last picture. We huddled, arms across shoulders, short girls in the front, tall girls crouching behind us to rest their chins on our shoulders. Mila wrapped her fingers around mine and gave me a squeeze; then, she grabbed Claire in a headlock. James tried to keep some personal space, but Blythe wrapped her arm around James' hip and jerked her into the frame. Blythe raised the phone and snapped the selfie. She examined the photo with a smile.

"How did we do it?" she asked. "Got a perfect pic on the first try."

She locked her phone and dropped it in the bag.

"You aren't going to post the pic first?" asked James.

"Nah," Blythe said. "It's for us. The internet doesn't have to see *everything*."

River snorted. "Since when?" she asked.

"Since right now," said Blythe. She opened the Tesla's passenger door and disappeared into the car to hide her HELLO bag under the seat. Her legs flailed in the air. Her stacked heel booties came dangerously close to marring the white leather on the open door. Blythe's commitment to fashion amazed me, but she'd be begging Claire to carry her around the carnival piggyback within minutes.

Knowing Claire, she'd probably do it too.

Blythe popped out of the car with her familiar star-shaped flask in hand. She chugged the contents and tossed it over her shoulder into the car.

"What was that?" asked Lolly.

"Apple juice," said Blythe, rolling her eyes. "What else would it be? Now come on, ladies, let's boogie."

We crossed the dark parking lot and stopped at the front gate. A massive gold apple statue stood outside the entrance. A giant had taken a big bite from the top, and a skull smiled back from the peeling skin. A plaque on the apple's concrete platform read:

POISON APPLE HALLOWEEN CARNIVAL
EST. JULY 24TH, 1922

James, River, and Gracie sat on the platform while Claire loudly debated strategy with herself.

"It makes the most sense to pair off based on location," she said. "The circus peanuts complicate things. Lolly and Violet can't go off by themselves. They're lightweights. They'll wind up dead." She turned to River. "We seriously should've waited on the edibles until after."

"Spilled milk, Toots," said River.

Claire stuck her hand in River's face. "Don't interrupt me. Cards! Give me your cards!"

River took a step back and said, "Whatever you say, Cap'n,"

We handed our cards over to Claire. She shuffled through the stack and laid them in a grid on the ground.

"Are you sure we shouldn't go alone and meet at the carousel in twenty?" asked Gracie.

"No. The carnival spans like, miles. There's no way some of you are going to collect your items and get back in twenty minutes, and I don't want anyone alone when the weed kicks in. Give me a second to do some mental math."

Claire nibbled her lip as she stared at the cards. My eyes went from her to the cards, to her, back to the cards. Blythe stood next to her, doing the same thing as me. A moment passed. Blythe got testy.

"This shouldn't be so hard," she said. She stumbled forward and placed a toe on my card. She wavered slightly. I gasped and leaned in to catch her, but she caught herself. Blythe used her toe to push the cards around into pairs. She pointed at Gracie and said, "River and Gracie, you're together. The House of Mirrors and Axe Throw are super close. James, you take Lolly over to the dunk tank, then head over to the test your strength game. They're on opposite sides, but they're both at the front of the carnival. Violet can come with me, and Mila and Claire are a team. Questions, comments, concerns?"

We all said no, except Lolly, who raised her hand.

"Dude," said James. "This isn't school. You don't need to raise your hand."

Lolly frowned. "How are we getting through the gate?"

"Excellent question," said Claire. "Check the note at the bottom of my invite." She handed it to Lolly.

"Employee entrance is faulty, opens from the inside without a key. Voila!" Lolly read.

"The employee entrance is over there," Claire said, pointing at a narrow door fifty feet away, near the guard stand. "Mila, I'll give you a boost, then you go open the door and let us in."

Claire knelt and held her hands out for Mila's foot. Gracie stopped them before Claire could launch Mila into the air.

"Uh, did y'all take a good look at the gate there?" she asked. "Those points at the top look sharp."

An elongated teardrop topped each iron bar. The bars were only four or five inches apart, and they were slick with dew.

Mila placed one foot on the low rung of the gate and gave it a shake. Water droplets showered her.

"It'll be fine," she said. "I can climb it without touching those spikes. Claire, let's do this."

Claire nodded. She grunted and flexed her muscles to lift Mila, who jumped high enough to grab the top bar. She did a pull-up and swung herself onto the top of the gate, where she squatted like a gargoyle and peered at us.

"You okay?" I asked.

"These things are like razors!" she said. "I cut the rubber on my sneaker!"

"Climb down before you cut more than your shoe!" River yelled.

Mila kicked her feet, swung through the air, and landed on her feet inside the gate.

"If I tried to do that, I'd break my neck," James mumbled in my ear.

"Same," I said.

Mila tiptoed past the guard stand and gave the door a push. It opened with no resistance.

"No security guard and a broken door," River said. "It's like they're asking people to break in."

"Where *is* the guard?" asked Lolly. Her eyes shifted left to right. She hadn't forgotten about her potential arrest.

James closed the door behind us. "He's probably jerking off in the House of Horrors or something. Stay in the shadows, and you won't get caught."

"What about security cameras?" I asked.

Every head turned to James. She sighed.

"Let me check," she said.

We found the door to the guard stand unlocked. James and I went inside. There were two flatscreen monitors, each divided into a grid displaying multiple shots from cameras all over the carnival. James sat in a rolling chair, spun around, and attacked the keyboard.

"I'm shutting them off," she said.

"Is there footage of us breaking in?" I asked.

"Probably. It can be erased. There isn't a ton of space on the hard drive. I doubt they save the footage. It won't be missed."

She clacked away, swiveling and fidgeting the whole time.

"Are you okay?" I asked.

"The peanut is hitting me," she said.

"Isn't it a bit soon? I don't feel anything."

"Maybe my metabolism is faster."

I laughed. "Are you calling me fat?"

"Yes. I did eat a higher dose than you, though. That's probably why."

"Are you going to be okay?" I asked.

"I have to be. Poor Lolly is going to lose her mind."

"Be nice to her," I said. "This is her first time."

"I'm aware. Don't worry. I'll watch her, we'll be fine, blah blah blah. Anyway, check this out."

She pointed at one of the screens. A hundred buttons blinked at us.

"The whole carnival is online," she said. "You can control the rides and lights and stuff from here. It's a pretty sophisticated system."

"Did you know before?" I asked. "Is this a problem?"

"No. It doesn't matter. I can turn the switches off along with the cameras. If the guard comes back, he'll spend his time getting the system back online instead of hunting us."

She clacked on the keyboard. Both monitors went dark. James gave the chair a few final spins and jumped to her feet. "All good," she said.

"Okay," I said. I peered through the window. Lolly swayed with her arms folded across her chest. River and Gracie played hopscotch on the blank pavement. Blythe flipped her hair to the wrong side and fluffed it. Claire stretched, prepping like she was about to run a marathon.

"We'll meet at the carousel, yes?" I asked.

"Yes, ma'am," James said. "Forty-five minutes from now, an hour tops."

She raised her hand to give me a high five. I slapped it too hard. She screeched and wrung her wrist.

"Save your energy for the hunt," she said.

CHAPTER 9

B lythe grabbed me and held me in place. She smelled like she'd used Jack Daniels for perfume.

"Let them go," she slurred. "I don't want Claire to see us."

"See us what?" I asked.

"I'm not following the gate and sneaking in shadows. We're going to go straight through the carnival."

I breathed a sigh of relief. We had to walk father than the others, easily a mile. If we went around, we'd add a mile to our hike. The carnival was dark enough that I wasn't worried about the lone security guard tracking us, should he ever show up. We stepped into the moonlight and headed for the carousel. Blythe tripped over her own feet, but I caught her before she hit the ground.

"You sure you're okay?" I asked.

"I'm fine," she said. "Look."

Blythe stood straight and touched the tip of her nose with each pointer finger, and walked a straight line, heel to toe. She swayed a bit, but she managed to stay upright for about six feet. She asked if I wanted her to say the alphabet backward.

"Can you say the alphabet backward while sober?" I asked.

Blythe narrowed her eyes. She didn't answer right away. I leaned in, waiting, watching her eyes slide in slightly different directions.

"No," she said finally. She opened her mouth to say more. No words came out.

"I can't believe we're here," I said, changing the subject. "Remember Freshman year? We talked about being chosen for the hunt. It's so surreal." I started walking again. Fortunately, she followed.

"You excited for school to start?" she asked.

"Honestly? No. Maybe if I knew about college. I feel like I'm walking a tightrope without a net."

"I feel you." Blythe held her arms out as though she were keeping her balance while walking on a wire.

"You have a net, though, right?" I asked. "When school is over, you get to focus entirely on your career."

Blythe snorted. "My *career*. I pretend to be a perfect goofball for the internet and get paid for it. I'm not a doctor or lawyer or anything. I'm not even a professional comedian. When I make something funny, it's by accident."

Her voice was flat, almost sad.

Maybe she was pretending to be perfect in real life too.

"A million years ago, back in elementary, we had to do drawings of our future selves," I told her. "Doctors, lawyers teachers, you know the drill. I already knew I wanted to play music. Professional musician wasn't a real job in my mind, so I drew myself in a Belldam Tower uniform. Our teacher walked around, and when she saw mine, she asked me to tell her about it. I said I wanted to work at my mom's hotel. She said I seemed upset about it. I told her yes, I was. I didn't want to work in a hotel and wear a uniform. I wanted to be a musician, but everyone else had drawn real jobs. Then she said something that always stuck with me. 'Violet, someone has to play music. Why not you? Besides, most of your friends won't be doctors and lawyers. Your minds will change as you get older. I bet a lot of you will do jobs that don't even exist yet. The world moves fast. There's always something new.'"

"We had the same lesson in my class," Blythe mumbled. "My picture was a puppy. That's what I wanted to be. A dog." She paused, stretched, and cracked her neck. "Maybe there's still time."

I laughed. "My point is, what you do now didn't exist when we were little. You're one of the kids she was talking about. You say it's not a real job. What does your bank account say?"

"Ugh. I don't want to talk about this anymore."

"Fair enough. Conversation dead and buried. Back to the task at hand: Do you want to go left past the House of Horrors or right past the House of Mirrors?"

"Right. There's a bathroom if we go that way, and I have to pee so bad I think I might burst." She did a little pee dance to show the direness of her situation.

"Too much apple juice?" I asked slyly.

She snorted. "Too much whiskey."

I extended a hand and allowed Blythe to lead the way. The moon made us a dimly lit, gray path, barely putting off enough light to cast our shadows on the ground. She stomped her long legs like a model on a runway. I shuffled at her heels.

We ducked into the dark bathroom. I ran my hand along the wall until I found the switch. The lights sizzled, blinking on, bathing the room in too bright blue-white light.

"I'm good," I said. "I'll keep watch outside."

"You should at least try to pee," she said. "My mom's number one rule. You never know if you'll get stuck without a bathroom when you need it."

"Fine."

I went into the accessible stall and pulled down my pants. Sure enough, I did have to go. I was slightly embarrassed for Blythe to hear me, so I held it in and waited for her to finish. Despite her overflowing bladder, Blythe managed to be completely silent. She flushed, then turned on the sink to wash her hands.

As soon as she turned on the water, I relaxed and peed as quietly as possible.

When I stepped out of the stall, the faucet was running, but Blythe was gone. I bent over to check for her feet under the stall doors. She wasn't there.

"Blythe?" I called out. "You still here?"

She didn't respond. I halfheartedly ran my hands under the water. The paper towel dispenser was empty, so I rubbed them dry on my jeans. My fingers brushed the light switch, but I decided to leave it on. Even if I wasn't staying in the bathroom, the little bright spot in the dark carnival comforted me. The blackness creeped me out more than I wanted to admit.

I turned the knob and pushed on the bathroom door with my shoulder. It didn't budge.

"What the hell?" I said aloud.

I twisted the knob harder. This time it turned, but the door didn't budge. I slammed my body into it a couple of times until it finally cracked open. I could see an inch of night. The door refused to open any further.

"Blythe?" I whispered through the crack. "Are you out there?"

She didn't answer. I let the door go, allowing it to close.

I paced a little, my head spinning. I wasn't usually claustrophobic, but edible induced paranoia hit me, and the ceiling lowered as the walls closed in. I hit the door with a fist and screamed for help. When I didn't get an immediate answer, I flipped out, slapping the door and grunting unintelligibly. I stuck my hand in the opening, my fingers disappearing into the darkness, and slammed my hip into the door until I pried it open wide enough to jam my foot in the space. Then slowly, a millimeter at a time, I jimmied the door back and forth until I twisted around and sucked my stomach in enough to slip out of the bathroom. The door scraped shut behind me.

"Ungh," I groaned. My muscles throbbed from squeezing through the tight space.

With the door closed, the light disappeared. I squatted to examine the ground to investigate how I'd gotten locked in. My fingers fumbled along the concrete until they found the culprit. I yanked it free and brought it into the moonlight.

It was a wet, rolled up, folded copy of our local paper, *The Belldam Bell*. It had gotten jammed under the door and had served as a doorstop. I threw it into a nearby trash can. It left my hand caked in mud, and moisture crept under my Hello Kitty bandaid. I peeled it off and threw it away as well. My cut still stung a little, but the bleeding had stopped hours earlier.

Blythe was nowhere to be found. I searched the immediate area, hoping to find her sprawled on the ground waiting for me or wandering in the open space by the carousel.

But she wasn't there. She wasn't anywhere.

"Blythe?" I whisper-yelled. I didn't dare raise my voice too loud. When she didn't answer, a tiny jolt of panic made the hair on my arms stand on end. I walked toward the House of Mirrors, still quietly calling her name.

My head felt light. My brain threatened to inflate until it cracked my skull. The circus peanut had begun to take effect, no question. Panic set in. I wouldn't be able to navigate to the Ferris wheel in the dark if I got too high.

Then, as if on cue, a loud crack echoed through the carnival and the lights switched on. A deep, demonic laugh boomed from the House of Horrors, drowning out the cheerful song from the carousel. Bright bulbs lit the arcade, and strobes flashed in the distance. A prerecorded voice boomed, "Step right up! Test your strength! Only muscle men need apply!"

Somewhere, far across the carnival, a shrill scream rang out until it abruptly stopped, switching off as quickly as the lights had switched on. I didn't recognize the voice, but it was female, and most likely, one of my friends.

Suddenly the light wasn't so comforting anymore.

CHAPTER 10

"Gotta move," Blythe mumbled to herself. "If I stop, it's over. I'm dead."

Greasy vomit rose in her throat. She regretted eating the nasty fried chicken at dinner and cursed herself for not being able to eat one stupid meal without posting it online.

She walked along the gate slowly, then when the power turned on, she picked up the pace. Her head felt light. Pure adrenaline powered her body. The carnival rotated around her, the lights spun faster and faster until they were as bright as the sun.

Someone screamed. Blythe stopped cold. Whoever it was, they were far away. Based on the direction of the scream, it was probably Mila, maybe River or Gracie.

Violet was still back at the bathroom. Blythe thought she heard her calling out. They'd run into each other again soon. Right now, she needed to be alone.

Ahead of her, tiny explosions inside a Paulie's Pop-a-Corn cart filled the air with a salty, buttery aroma. She was surprised. It made sense for the rides to power on, but not the popcorn machines. She wondered if the other food stands turned on automatically, and inhaled deeply. The distinct scent of burnt sugar and warm peanuts made her stomach turn. It would be a miracle if she kept the fried chicken down.

"God, I really don't want to be here," she said aloud. "The fucking carousel music. It's gonna be stuck in my head for days."

Once upon a time, she loved the carnival. Before the divorce, she would come every December with her dad when they did a Winter Wonderland overlay on the carnival. It was the only place in Belldam where you could see snow. There was a vast swath of land in the back corner where the staff loaded in piles and piles of the fake stuff for guests to build snowmen and have epic snowball fights. She and her dad would get sugared up on hot chocolate flavored cotton candy and fall in the faux snow to make angels.

Nowadays, she barely got a phone call on Christmas. There were always plenty of gifts to open, but there hadn't been snow angels in years.

Thoughts of her father made her chest hurt. This wasn't the time to cry. This was the night she'd waited for. Blythe pictured a lit candle, focused on the flame. Her therapist taught her that trick. She forgot about her dad, about the chicken, about the carousel music. When her mind was clear, she blew out the candle and opened her eyes.

She needed a place to regroup, somewhere along the midway. Lolly and James would be there. She desperately needed to find them.

Her black shoes crunched in the gravel. Her head felt unbearably hot, and the humid air made it almost impossible to breathe without choking. She should've worn shorts. She wished she could text her friends. It would be so much easier to find them.

"This isn't nearly as fun as I imagined it would be," she said to herself. "This night needs to end. In an hour, the hunt will be over. One hour and I'll be done. Sixty little minutes. That's it."

Someone else's shoes crunched in the gravel. Lightning shot up her spine, shocking her out of her skin. She leaped out of sight and pressed her body against the cold gate.

As the dark figure approached, Blythe pulled herself together. It was a friend. It had to be. She just couldn't tell which one.

She gulped for air, then stepped directly into the path of the oncoming person.

Her head spun again, and as the person's face came into focus, her vision blurred until the whole world went black.

CHAPTER 11

We learned about the fight or flight response in Science. Our lessons left out the third option: freeze.

I read about it in an article on women's self-defense. I asked my mom why no one ever mentioned freezing. She told me to Google it; she was busy with a project for work. Instead, I asked James what she thought.

"Probably because people like to think they can survive a dangerous situation. It's a control thing. Like, any choice they might make could lead to the defeat of their attacker," she said. "Plus, it gives dickheads a reason to judge victims."

"What do you mean?" I asked.

She put on a condescending voice. "Jane Doe deserved what she got. A maniac with a chainsaw ran at her, and she stood there. I'd never do that. I'd run and never look back."

When I watched horror movies, I would imagine Samara crawling from my TV or Leatherface on my doorstep. I'd definitely run. Who wouldn't?

But when the carnival sprang to life, and a scream ripped through the night, I froze.

My mind raced as I calculated my next move:

Something is not right here.

Where is Blythe?

Who turned on the lights?

Who screamed?

Does the popcorn machine really start when the power goes on? Why is that necessary?

I should find Blythe. She can't have gotten far.

Has the security guard found us?

What if he called the cops?

Where is everyone else?

I should call out. Someone will answer.

Why isn't anyone else calling out?

What if everyone is dead?

Why do I automatically assume people are dead?

We're more likely to be arrested than murdered.

I should walk toward the scream.

I should run away from the scream.

I should hide to see if this tides over.

My gut pulled me toward Blythe. My feet pulled me to hide. My brain told them both to shut up as it drew me to the center of the carnival. The others would be there or close by. We could find Blythe together. It was stupid to split up in the first place, and I wouldn't be making that mistake again.

I snuck along the alley behind the arcade; my body pressed against the plywood exterior. I did my best to run between the shadows, ducking, and pausing after each step. When I turned the corner, I saw Lolly, still as a statue next to the Black Kitten Coaster, as frozen as I'd been minutes before.

"Lolly." I called softly. "Lolly."

She stared at the Black Kitten Coaster's worm shaped buggies. Her hand drifted to the little gate like she might push it open to hide inside.

Emboldened by the knowledge that I wasn't alone, I sprinted toward her. I said her name again, this time at full volume. Her head shot up, and she flashed a smile.

She never saw him coming.

A black fabric swirl appeared behind Lolly, as though the monster had manifested from thin air. It wrapped one gloved hand around her throat, holding her tight in a headlock. Lolly was too stunned to fight back, her mind melted by the edible.

I screamed, and the monster looked at me.

I recognized him immediately.

Each October, the carnival had a massive Halloween celebration.

Somehow the staff managed to make the already spooky carnival into an over the top, almost gratuitous celebration.

They covered everything in spider webs, including the poor ticket takers. Thousands of pumpkins got hauled in to be carved by world-famous carving artists. The deep fry carts, which already sold death-defying treats as a matter of course, sold even weirder stuff like fake fried blood and *very* realistic fried rats.

Special events call for seasonal employees, and it felt like management intentionally chose the creepiest applicants to help set the mood: close talkers, touchy-feely men, ride operators who asked too many personal questions. Sorry, Mr. Mirror Maze Man, it's none of your business what my first crush's lips tasted like.

Yuck.

Worst of all were the scare actors, not because they were creepy, but because they seemed dangerous.

From September to mid-November, a portion of the carnival turned into a free-range haunt. People in costumes followed and harassed you, jumped in your face to yell, that kind of thing. They had ultra realistic weapons, and their covered faces emboldened them to swing them a little too close to carnival guests.

Even so, on good nights when the actors were energized and well behaved, it was fun to walk around feeling free to scream as loud as you wanted when a zombie or haunted doll lumbered after you. It was a safe release, and for a few hours, I could turn my brain off and live a little. A thirst for those nights kept me coming back year after year.

The previous October, James packed me, Blythe, River, Gracie, and Ever Best, River's art geek friend, into Heather's van and headed to the outskirts of town.

As soon as we entered the carnival, two scarecrows with chainsaws chased us toward the midway. We screeched and ran, bursting into laughter next to the ring toss. James took my hand, and I took Ever's, then River joined the chain, then Gracie, with Blythe bringing up the rear.

We locked into our daisy chain any time we walked through the scare actor zones. Scare actors patrolled the area between the midway and the arcade. Anything past the House of Horrors was out of bounds. For the most part, they swarmed the merry-go-round, terrorizing anyone who answered the calliope's siren song.

We unlinked at the food court. River had the munchies and wanted a hot dog. Ever wanted some slime lime cotton candy. James needed to pee.

Blythe and I stood next to the spinning Crazy Cauldrons, bitching about the cold. We noticed a scare actor staring at us from a distance but didn't react. We were well beyond his boundaries.

He edged forward a bit, stomping a wide stride, his gloved hand gripping a realistic looking axe.

"Is he coming over here?" I asked.

Blythe looped her arm in mine. "Maybe we know him," she said. "Most of the actors go to Pritchett. I bet it's River's ex, Brogan Whatshisname."

"Ooh, I bet. He's basically stalking her."

"Well, I welcome him to come to me," Blythe said, her voice raised. "I'll kick his fucking ass!"

The actor heard her and picked up the pace until he flew

toward us at a full speed run. He passed a clump of people, shoving a girl in a pink cowboy hat into the mud. Blythe squeezed my arm.

As he got closer, I could see his costume in better detail. His rubber mask was one of the more grotesque ones I'd seen on a scare actor. It was a coal black demon face, with elongated bloodshot eyes and a shiny finish that made the skin appear to ooze.

The demon's tongue was the worst part. Pale gray-pink, hanging limply down his chest. When he shook his head, the tongue flopped side to side, making him look like he was salivating to slurp us right up.

I braced for impact. He stopped short of crashing into us. He pushed me to the side and pressed his chest against Blythe. He was a little taller than her with the mask on, though not tall enough to intimidate her. He shoved her into the concrete barrier surrounding the Crazy Cauldrons.

"What is wrong with you?" Blythe asked, pushing him away.

"Pretty," he whispered. "Pretty pretty."

"Get off her!" I yelled. Faces turned in our direction, curious people wondering if they were witnessing a show.

The actor turned toward me and slammed the axe into the ground at my feet. The blade stuck into the ground and stood at attention.

Scare actors weren't supposed to have real, sharp weapons.

Cold sweat rolled down my face.

"So pretty," he said. He cradled Blythe's chin and rested his forehead against hers. The tongue threatened to dip into her shirt, right between her boobs.

"Get off me, or I'm going to scream, you asshole," Blythe said through gritted teeth. "And I mean a losing my shit scream, full-on bloody murder. My friend will too."

The actor slammed his fist into the wall, only an inch or two away from Blythe's head. She winced. My fingers curled into claws. I was ready to rip the mask off and shove it down his throat.

With little fanfare, he backed off, pulled his axe from the dirt, and wandered back into the designated scare actor zone.

"Whaaaaat the hell was that?" I asked.

"No idea," she said. She pulled on her shirt where the tongue had been, making sure she wasn't exposed. "Maybe he's a fan. Or maybe he hate watches my videos. Or maybe he's a jerk who gets off on harassing cute girls who look like easy targets. I don't think it was Brogan. He's terrified of me ever since he hit on me, and I told him to die in a pile of fire ants. No way that pussy is The Licker."

"The Licker?" I laughed. "That's the name you're going with?"

"What else you gonna call something with that tongue?"

Past Blythe whispered in my ear as the masked man threw Lolly around like a rag doll.

"The Licker," she said. *"What else?"*

Lolly's face turned purple. She weakly fought back, limply slapping his arms. He didn't even flinch.

I screamed, losing my shit, full-on bloody murder. The Licker dragged Lolly backward, almost out of sight. This time my brain let my body take charge, and my body wanted to fight.

The Licker was ready when I slammed into him. He didn't miss a beat; he had me on the ground before I even threw a punch. I searched for a weapon but didn't see any nearby. The Licker didn't like how mobile I was, so he kicked his black sneaker into my chest twice. It knocked the wind out of me. I panicked when I couldn't catch my breath.

Lolly had gone limp. He dropped her and dragged her across the gravel. At first, I thought he was taking her into the arcade so they'd be alone, and he could do whatever he wanted in private.

But he kept going and dragged her to the test your strength booth.

The giant measuring stick at the back of the booth stood ten feet in the air. A bell hung at the top, a puck sat at the bottom, a metal plate laid in front. The player would slam a mallet into the plate, and the puck would shoot up to ring the bell.

The Licker threw Lolly on the ground. She rolled away, far enough to piss him off, not far enough to escape. She screamed my name.

"I'm coming!" I groaned through gasps.

He grabbed her shoulders and pounded her back into the ground. Her neck snapped, her head lolled from side to side. She fought as best she could; he was too strong. He head-butted her so hard I could practically hear their skulls bang together. He gently lowered her head onto the plate.

One summer, when I was little, my family stayed at the beach for a week in a massive hotel in Corpus Christi. My cousins Cory and Brett had their own room on the fourth floor, overlooking the pool. The boys managed to sneak into the pastry kitchen and stole some watermelons. Strangely, not a single staff member questioned the sight of two massively pregnant teenage boys roaming the hotel halls.

My cousins sent me to the ground floor to be the lookout. Though they were dumb enough to toss watermelons four stories onto the pavement, they were smart enough to understand someone walking under them could get hurt.

I was excited to be included.

Brett, my oldest cousin, had the bigger watermelon. He raised it over his head and slammed it as hard as he could. I'd expected it to crack like in half like an egg. Instead, it exploded. Juice and pink goo flew through the air hard enough to make me flinch when it hit me in the face. The rind broke apart into a dozen big chunks. The largest piece caved in on itself, vomiting up more of the pink meat inside.

When The Licker slammed the weighted mallet on Lolly's

head, I saw the watermelon. Her skin was the rind, her bones the thick white lining, her brains and blood the sweet pink meat. Some teeth landed at The Licker's feet.

"They're the seeds," I whispered.

My face was warm and wet. Lolly's beautiful brain sprayed across my shirt in a lovely abstract pattern. Her body lay limp, nearly within my reach.

The Licker left the mallet on her face. He walked toward me, close enough to see the slight shimmer in his cheap Halloween store cloak. I closed my eyes. Lolly was dead; it was my turn now.

He dropped onto one knee in front of me. He leaned forward and pressed his tongue to my cheek. My mind flashed back to October, to Blythe and the rubber tongue on her chest.

He breathed a muffled wheeze inside the mask. Hot air blew through the mesh guard over his mouth.

"Hi, Violet," he said. Some kind of electronic device disguised his voice. "Remember me?"

I pulled away, squeezing my eyes shut until fireworks appeared on the inside of my lids. He leaned closer. I braced for his touch.

Without warning, he stood. I opened my eyes. He gave me a little wave. The Licker turned and ran, kicking up a cloud of dust behind him.

I looked over at Lolly's dead body. It jumped, one last twitch from her muscles before she never moved again.

CHAPTER 12

When I caught my breath, I ran toward the entrance. I figured anyone who heard my screams would've decided to get the hell away from the carnival.

My assumptions were incorrect. Claire stood paralyzed in front of the photo printing shop, out in the open, fixated on the pretty lights on the Whirling Witch Coaster.

"It's like a postcard," she said. "They made it look so real." She turned to face me. Her pupils were the size of saucers.

My edible hadn't affected me as much as hers had...or so I thought. I'd been too preoccupied running for my life to realize the world seemed a little worn around the edges. But now, next to Claire, I felt myself slipping away.

I grabbed Claire and gave her a good shake.

"Lolly is dead!" I cried. "There is someone in a black hooded cloak and demon mask. I've seen it before. It's a scare actor costume from the carnival at Halloween. Blythe named him The Licker. We have to get outta here."

Claire tilted her head. "What's on your shirt?" she asked, pulling at the hem.

"Lolly," I told her. "Lolly is on my shirt. Now come on, we have to go!"

I grabbed her hand and pulled her toward the exit. She stood firm. Claire was 140 pounds of solid muscle. I, on the other hand, could barely help our orchestra director move a cello.

"We. Can't. Leave. Them," she said dreamily.

"Yes, we can! We'll get out and go to Blythe's car and get our phones and call 911. We won't be able to help the others if we're dead."

"No. No, that won't do at all. Did you ever read the one book we were supposed to read in English? Something something no man left behind."

"I have no idea what you're talking about. Claire, we gotta go."

"No, listen to me. Listen." She paused and stared back up at the Whirling Witch Coaster. "They might not even know they're in danger. Mila screamed earlier when the lights came on. No one noticed."

"*I* noticed. That's why I made the stupid decision to find you guys. It didn't work out, now Lolly is freaking *dead*, and if we don't leave this carnival, so are we."

"Lolly is dead?" Claire asked, suddenly alert.

"I hope so, or it's going to take a lot of surgery to reconstruct her head."

Claire pushed me away. "If you want to leave, go. I'll get you outside the gate, and then you can run to Blythe's car. If the doors don't open, keep running to the subdivision behind the woods. Scream your head off once you're in the clear. I'm going to try to find the others."

"Claire," I said flatly. "You're high as shit. You can't go looking for them alone."

"I'm not so high that I can't outrun this guy, maybe even take him down. My last training session, I deadlifted 230 pounds."

"Is 230 a lot?"

Claire gave me a side-eye. "Yes, bitch. It's a lot."

Claire wasn't always an athlete.

One night, at a sleepover, she and I were the only two girls still awake. We went outside and laid in the driveway, staring at the starless sky. We talked about everything from my missing dad to her desire to adopt and train a Rottweiler. I'd brought brownie bites with me and offered her one. She declined and told me a story.

For a long time, she was so skinny every bone in her body poked through her skin. People would stare at her when her parents took her out, whispering that Mr. and Mrs. Smithson must be abusing their daughter. They took her to the doctor, who declared Claire was a perfectly healthy girl who just needed to eat more.

"Put sweetened condensed milk in her oatmeal," the doctor said. "She will get nice and chubby."

Claire's parents were at the end of their rope, so they bought sweetened condensed milk and gave Claire three bowls of oatmeal a day in addition to her regular meals. The excess sugar made Claire's eyes bulge, made her throat burn, and kept her on the edge of nausea all day long, but she kept quiet and did her best not to puke because she didn't want to upset her parents.

She suffered through the oatmeal until one Mother's Day when her Grandma Stephanie came to visit. When Stephanie saw her son prepare sweetened condensed milk spiked oatmeal for her Claire, she flipped out.

"What are you feeding your child?" Stephanie asked.

"Her pediatrician said this would make her gain weight."

"It's also going to give her diabetes! She's as skinny as ever, and she's shaky and sweaty! You need to take her to another doctor, Jason, and you need to do it today."

After a brief fight - he told his mother he knew how to raise his kid; she said it was crazy to feed sugar syrup to a nine year old - he relented and allowed her to call around to see if another pediatrician could fit Claire in. One had an open spot, and her dad took her in.

It turned out Claire didn't need to eat more food. She needed medicine because her thyroid was out of whack. The doctor wrote a prescription and gave a stern order to stop feeding Claire sugary food to fatten her up.

Six months later, medicine combined with a healthy diet changed Claire's body for the better. She finally had enough energy to play with other kids, and she begged her dad to enroll her in swimming lessons.

"The first time I hit the pool, I almost drowned," she told me. "I sank. I wasn't scared, though. My swim teacher fished me out, handed me a kickboard, and I fluttered around in the water like a fish until I was a raisin. If I could live in the water, I would."

"Like me and the violin," I said. I took another brownie from my bag and ate half. "Is that why you don't eat brownies? A training diet for swimming?"

"Hell no," she laughed. "I'll pig out on anything salty, spicy, or sour. It's just after the oatmeal... I'd rather die than eat anything sweet."

I squeezed Claire's hand, and we prepared to make our run for the little door in the gate. We hadn't even taken a step when the lights around us cut off.

My eyes couldn't adjust to the dark. Everything was black, so black that I couldn't make out the shapes around us. My body felt light like I might float away. I was a balloon, tethered to the earth by Claire's weirdly rough hand.

A scratchy electronic screech ripped through the night. Claire wrapped her arms around our heads to block the sound.

"Lolly pop, oh lolly pop," sang a demonic voice. "Hey, Violet, wanna gimme some sugar?"

I slid from Claire's arms and crawled under her legs.

"What is going on?" I whispered. "Where is he?"

"I don't …will you please get off the ground? You're going to drag me down with you."

Across the carnival, near the House of Horrors, lights flashed on and off.

"Look!" I gasped.

"Is that where the killer is?" Claire asked.

"Not necessarily. James told me computers control the power. If anything, he's in the security office." I paused, remembering our conversation with Mr. Luzon. "There *was* supposed to be a guard here tonight, wasn't there?"

Claire nodded. "I'll bet you a shiny nickel Ned ain't guarding anything tonight."

"I thought his name was Fred? Or was it Frank?"

"I don't know, Violet. It's not like I'm friends with the dude. Ugh. I'm dizzy." Claire squeezed the bridge of her nose. "Wait. His name was definitely Floyd. Or maybe Ralph."

"Do you think The Licker got Ralph?" I asked, pulling at her legs.

She lifted me to my feet and coaxed me behind a recycling bin. We crouched in the dirt to debate.

"We can't go back to the entrance," she said. "If *The Licker* is running the lights from the security office, we'd have to walk right past him."

"I like how you say *The Licker* like it's a ridiculous name. He's got a ten inch long rubber tongue he likes to rub on people."

"Gross."

"Exactly."

"Okay," she said, her tone harsh. "We're going the long way around to the House of Horrors. We'll stay close to the structures and avoid the lights if they come on again."

I sighed, slightly relieved.

"Are we going to make it out alive?" I asked.

"Sure," Claire said. She dropped her voice to a whisper. "Or die trying."

CHAPTER 13

When the power came back on, Mila was unprepared. She stood out in the open, feeling naked. Something wasn't right. The screams she'd heard across the carnival weren't from surprise. They were from terror.

She kicked herself for losing Claire. If anyone could keep them safe, it would be her. But when the carnival lit up, and the screaming started, she ran, and Claire didn't follow. By the time Mila realized they'd been separated, there was no way to find her.

Mila ducked into the midway. The ring toss had a big prize wall displaying stuffed animals, a perfect hiding place. She climbed into the booth and made a fort out of teddy bears. They brushed softly against her skin. Thanks to the circus peanuts, the sensation mesmerized her, and she couldn't help but stroke their silky fur with her cheek.

Footsteps crunched in the dirt. Mila froze. She didn't breathe, didn't even blink. She peeped through the toys as best she could. If it were one of the other girls, she would crawl out and grab her friend and never let go.

It wasn't a friend.

A tall figure dressed in all black walked past the ring toss booth. Or rather, he stalked past with his shoulders hunched, his pace slow. He barely picked up his feet at all. He stopped at a Paulie's Pop-A-Corn cart across from her and knocked a stack of red and white striped popcorn boxes on the ground. Mila gasped.

The figure whipped around. His comically long rubber tongue flopped back and forth. Mila shut her eyes and prayed to God that she wouldn't laugh at the sight of him. She always got the giggles with weed. When her grandfather died, she was so distraught all she wanted was to stop feeling her feelings. One phone call to River got her a fat baggie filled with gummy bears. She ate three before the funeral, and when the tiny old veterans stood to honor her grandfather, she could barely contain herself. "They're the munchkin gang," she whispered to her brother, Mikey. He'd had some gummies too. They spent the rest of the service gripping each other's arms so hard they'd left bruises.

The Licker's feet scraped the dirt as he walked to the ring toss booth. She squinted, opening her eyes just enough to see him hover over the counter. When she saw his demonic mask, she didn't need to hold back laughter. Instead, she held back a scream.

He stayed at the counter for about thirty seconds, but with her brain on stoner time and her inability to breathe without being heard, it felt like hours. Finally, he straightened his back, turned toward the heart of the midway, and walked away.

The stuffed animals didn't provide enough cover. Several body parts were dangerously close to being exposed. A shift in the wind would reveal her hiding spot. A little wooden shelf inside the counter hung a few feet away; it was her best shot at a hiding spot. Her body would barely fit, but as long as he didn't step inside the ring toss booth to look around, she'd be safe there.

She made herself as small as possible and slid out onto the dry dirt. She lowered herself onto her belly and slithered like a snake toward the shelf. Her palms and forearms scraped the dirt, stinging as the skin split. She'd have painful scrapes tomorrow.

She wondered if it would impact cheer practice.

When her hand touched wood, she flipped her body around and folded herself in half. She scooted sideways onto the shelf.

"I'm safe," she thought.

She was wrong.

Black gloved fingers wrapped around the counter, mere inches from her head.

"Did you think I wouldn't see you?" he asked. His voice sounded garbled like a robot shoved underwater.

He pulled on the counter with one hand. It shook a little but didn't fall. He grabbed it with both hands and yanked hard. This time the whole counter moved. Cheap plywood cracked as the nails let go. The Licker summoned all his strength. The counter finally gave, and tipped over on top of him.

This was Mila's last chance. A broken shard of wood stuck up from the remnants of her shelf. She cracked it off and ran. It wasn't a great weapon, but it was something.

The midway had been the first structure built on the grounds of the carnival. In those days, there were six games, and each involved throwing various balls against targets. As demand grew, so did the desire for new games. First, a little bobbing for apples booth. Next came a pop gun booth where you could shoot little racing horses. The apple booth's owner didn't like guns, so they insisted the racing horse game be built several feet away. As more and more booths were erected, the layout became convoluted. There was no rhyme or reason, a turn around a corner could lead you down a dark corridor or dead end. It didn't help that multiple similarly named booths offered the same games, or that a dozen Pop-A-Corn stands made every row look identical to the last.

Mila knew better than to head deeper into the midway. The lights could go out again at any moment, and she'd be screwed. She took a left and ran toward the House of Horrors. Unfortunately, The Licker beat her to the punch.

He caught her by the hair and gave it a hard yank. She refused to go out without a fight. Her legs were strong enough to hold her on another girl's shoulders before doing a back somersault to land on a football field, a big bright smile never leaving her face. She kicked him in the chest, then in the crotch. She stabbed at him wildly with her stick. It slid into his skin; with all the wrestling, she couldn't tell what body part she'd penetrated. An electronic screech howled as he screamed in pain.

She hadn't done enough to stop him, only to anger him. He'd was done with their little scuffle. He threw her on the ground so hard her shoulder snapped, then he crawled on top of her, straddling her stomach.

"Get off me!" Mila yelled.

"Is this yours?" He took Mila's stick and scratched it across her neck. If he'd wanted to, he could've ended it all right there. A stake through the neck, not quite a vampiric death but pretty damn close.

That's not what The Licker wanted. He'd made plans over the past few months, good plans he didn't want to abandon. Shocking deaths for the best and brightest.

It's what they deserved.

Still, he needed her incapacitated. She would fight until her dying breath if she could. He hadn't yet had the pleasure of feeling a sharp object slide into soft skin. The wood pierced her shoulder with ease. He felt it tear through the muscle, maybe even felt it scrape bone. The pain overwhelmed Mila, sending her into shock.

The Licker threw her over his shoulder and walked her to a booth. Through bleary eyes she saw six plaster clown heads, their mouths gaping, ready to be filled. The closest clown had big red lips and a blue star over its left eye. It had been the one on her Scavenge invitation.

He laid her on the counter. She rolled toward him, landing inside the booth. He glanced at her and decided she was too weak to escape. She watched as he pulled back a curtain to reveal a hidden toolbox. Mila wanted to run, stand, or even pull herself into a sitting position, but the blood loss and clanging in her head kept her under his control.

The Licker reached into the box and produced two long nails and a hammer. He held them high for Mila to see. She moaned, blubbered, gasped for air. If she kept panicking, she'd do his job for him.

He put the hammer and nails on the little stool where the carnie sat when carnival traffic was slow. Then he propped Mila against the back wall between two weathered ceramic clown heads. He put her right hand above her head and placed a nail in her palm. Mila squirmed and begged for him to stop.

The Licker didn't listen.

The first time he struck the nail, it didn't go all the way through. To combat this, he hit it six more times until he was satisfied with his work.

Mila counted each hit in her head. After three, she went numb. He stepped back to admire his handiwork. She hung in place, her palm threatening to rip in half from supporting her weight, her legs dangling a few inches above the ground uselessly.

Mila never thought she'd be grateful for someone to hammer a nail into her flesh, but when The Licker gave the second nail three hard strikes into her other palm, it redistributed her weight and took some pressure off her right hand, providing her slight relief. She flexed her fingers as best she could. He'd done too good a job for her to move them much.

At seventeen, Mila had never spent much time worrying about her last moments. Her best guess was she'd die at ninety surrounded by her great-grandchildren in a sunny hospital room. If she had fantasized about dying young, she would've guessed her final thoughts would've been of her parents or her brother, maybe her boyfriend or her friends. Certainly she would've thought about cheerleading, the sport she'd loved since she took her first tumbling class in preschool.

It turns out, all she could think about was when, as a little kid, she stole some scissors and used them to cut quarter-inch baby bangs. It was her earliest memory. She didn't know why she'd done it, but she vividly remembered the snipping sound the blades made as they sliced through the hair, and the satisfying sprinkle of hair falling on the Sesame Street coloring book in her lap. Mila didn't notice The Licker pick up the water gun.

She screamed when he pressed it against her lips and shoved it past her teeth. He wasn't worried her friends would hear; the barrel of the gun muzzled her nicely. He pressed harder until it slid down her throat. She screamed louder, which pissed him off. He pulled the gun out and shoved it back into her throat, cracking several bottom teeth as he did it.

Mila could barely breathe. If he left her there, it would take a while for her to choke, but she'd surely be dead before sunup.

That wasn't his plan.

The Licker fondled the rubber hose connecting the gun to a massive water tank under the counter. Mila closed her eyes. The rusty knob creaked when he turned it. The hose kicked back a little as it filled with water. She focused on her memory of her self inflicted haircut. The Licker approached, pressing his body into hers. Her head rested on her shoulder. A familiar scent clung to his clothes. Floral. Expensive. She couldn't quite place it.

The gun clicked when he pulled the trigger. Water burst into her throat. It reminded The Licker of a bullfrog. He poked at her neck, amused at how it bounced like a water balloon when he flicked it.

Mila's body involuntarily gasped for air until the water filled her lungs. When she went limp, The Licker didn't release the trigger. Though she might've looked dead, he wasn't about to make assumptions. When the water had nowhere else to go, it rushed back up her throat into her mouth. It spewed all over her white t-shirt, revealing a baby blue bralette.

The Licker let the gun go. It remained stuck in her throat. He removed a glove and pressed his fingers to her neck. No pulse.

Before he put his glove back on, he checked his phone. It was already 1:30.

Two down, too many to go.

CHAPTER 14

Claire and I ducked behind a trash can when we heard heavy footsteps running toward us. She peeked around the side and watched The Licker sprint past.

"He went around the corner," she whispered. "Toward the Mirror Maze."

"River and Gracie," I said. "That's where they were supposed to be."

"I know."

In the distance, the lights on the Whirling Witch Coaster turned off. Behind us, the entrance lights blinked on and off for a moment until they lit up permanently. I shivered. There were eyes on me, a stranger close enough I could feel his breath on my neck. I whipped around, expecting to find myself nose to nose with his hideous mask.

No one was there.

"What if it's more than one person?" I asked. "One guy running around killing people and another controlling the lights."

"Plausible," Claire said. "This is good, though. He's running away from us, and the lights are on out front. He's probably turning on the lights for himself. It's a lot harder to chase girls when we're under cover of darkness. We can split up now."

I swear to God, I almost slapped her for her stupidity. *"No. Fucking. Way."*

I stared into her eyes, daring her to flinch. She picked at the hem of her shorts.

"Alright. We stay together and go in the opposite direction," she said. "Do you have a watch?"

"No. I have a phone," I said, rolling my eyes. "It has a clock."

"Do you have your phone with you?"

"...no."

"Then don't be a smart ass. I don't have one either. See the moon?" She pointed at the sky.

"Does the moon have a watch?" I asked. The idea of the moon unfolding his arms to check the time cracked me up.

"Are you too high to function?" Claire asked. I shook my head. "Good. It'll be straight above us soon. When it moves west above the woods, we're leaving whether we've found the other girls or not. Okay?"

"Mmmhmm." My body was so loose I couldn't even form words.

Claire led me toward the House of Horrors. It struck me as ironic we were planning to save ourselves from a killer by hiding in a haunted house. I tried to point this out to Claire. Instead, I told a rambling, incoherent story about a movie I'd watched the night before.

"They're trapped in this castle, and they can't leave," I said. "There's a monster. Then this girl comes. She hid in plain sight. He saw her. He didn't kill her. They danced a lot."

"You're describing *Beauty and the Beast*," Claire said. "That has nothing to do with right now."

"Remember when you said you were going to the movies, and instead you made out with Shiloh Curtis in Lolly's treehouse?"

"Why?"

"Shiloh kinda looks like the baby teapot because of her chipped front tooth she refuses to get fixed."

"Stop talking about *Beauty and the Beast*."

"Okay."

We were past the midway, almost to the carnival entrance when she held out an arm to stop me.

"Do you hear that?" she asked.

A tiny sound, like a mewling kitten, came from behind the fried Coke stand. Claire gave me some random hand signals I chose to ignore. She sighed and wrapped her fingers around my wrist. Her usually perfect manicure was marred; the peacock blue polish had half peeled off her stubby nails.

She gently pushed me to the left; she snuck around the right. We circled the stand ready to pounce. Claire jumped into place, eyes wild.

"Please don't hurt me!" Gracie yelped. She lay in a ball on her side, with her eyes smushed shut and her fingers in her ears. Her Edna Mode glasses had disappeared.

I breathed a sigh of relief and tapped her with my toe. "It's us."

Gracie relaxed and rolled onto her back. Claire pulled her to her feet.

"Have you seen him?" Gracie asked.

"Oh, we saw him. Violet especially saw him."

I nodded. "He talked to me."

"Whoa, whoa, whoa," said Claire. "That is some vital information you neglected to share. What did he say?"

"My name."

"You know him?" asked Gracie. "From where?"

"Here, maybe. Last October, when we came here with James and Blythe and River and Ever, there was a scare actor who cornered Blythe and acted gross."

"Oh my God," said Claire. "She said the guy's mask had a big floppy tongue. That's what the killer is wearing."

"Yeah," I said. "Something struck me as odd that night. He

had a real axe. No one else carried real weapons. He left the scare zone too. Went out of bounds."

"You think it's the same guy? Like he stalked her before, and now he's after all of us?" Claire asked.

"No," Gracie said. "Later Blythe found out the creepy guy did it on a dare. There were a few assholes who broke the rules and egged each other on to do stuff like bring real weapons and grope girls. One of the idiots stabbed himself with a real chef's knife. He ratted the others out to keep his job. They fired him anyway."

I vaguely recalled Blythe telling me that story.

"What if this is those guys out for revenge?" Claire asked.

"Maybe," I said. "Or maybe it's someone else. Maybe Mr. Luzon is pissed we threatened him, or a crazy Blythe fan snapped. Maybe the security guard is a sadist, and we walked into his playground. It could be anyone."

Claire rubbed her temples. "I'm less concerned with who he is and more concerned with getting out alive. We can let the cops play derective."

"Derective?" I asked.

"I said detective." Claire swayed a little, and her eyes went crossed.

"Between one to ten, how high is everyone right now?" I asked. "Don't lie."

"I'm fully at a six," said Gracie. "I'm okay until I hit eight. Right now it's enough to keep me from peeing my pants with fear, so that's good."

"Nine over here, bitches," laughed Claire. She held her arms above her head in triumph.

"Jesus, it's not a contest. I'm probably a three," I lied. In truth, I was closer to a five. Any more than that and I'd be toast. Lolly saved me when she asked me to split the candy.

A lump formed in my throat as I thought about her sweet apprehension at the weed.

"Where are the others? Violet, where's Blythe?"

I nodded. "We went to the bathroom, and she wandered off. She was wasted. Best case scenario, she passed out in a dumpster somewhere."

"I lost River when the lights came on." She pointed toward the Mirror Maze. "We were over there. What about James? Or Lolly?"

Claire and I glanced at each other. A tear rolled down Gracie's cheek.

"Lolly is dead," I said. "The Licker killed her."

"How?" Gracie asked.

"Not important."

"How?"

I swallowed. "He smashed her head with the mallet at the test your strength booth," I said.

Gracie turned away and vomited garlic bread grilled cheese sandwich on her shoes. I patted her on the back as she continued to heave. Her eyes rolled up at me. She gave a grateful half smile.

Then she noticed my shirt.

"Violet, what's all over you?" Gracie asked, knowing.

I paused. I told myself I wanted to save Gracie from the gory details. This was only half true. I also wanted to spare myself the trauma of reliving it. Even our conversation made me replay it in my head over and over. If I said the words, it made Lolly's death real, the mental movie would never end. Any time I heard her name from then on, I would picture watermelon.

Gracie pressed, and Claire nodded.

"I was next to her when she died," I said. "Her blood got all over me."

"There's spatters on your face."

"Yes."

Gracie scanned my front, pulling my shirt close to her weak eyes so she could get a clear view.

"Why is this blood chunky?"

I begged Claire for guidance with my eyes. She shrugged.

"Gracie," I said softly. "He hit her pretty hard. Have you ever seen a watermelon explode?"

Gracie jumped back and wailed. "Are those Lolly's brains. Is this really happening? Is this really fucking happening? Where is she? I can't look at a dead body. Tell me this is a joke. I won't be mad. I swear. Tell me it's a joke by the old Seniors. I don't care. Please. Please. *Please.*"

Claire bent down and covered Gracie's mouth. It muffled her ranting, but it didn't stop.

"She's still where he left her," Claire said through gritted teeth. "We aren't going over there. You're not going to see it. We're going to hide, and if he finds us, we're going to kill him."

"Kill him?" I asked, stunned.

Claire let Gracie go. "You think Lolly is his only target? This is us against him, and if I have to fight him, I'm playing for keeps."

My chest twitched, followed by the corners of my mouth. I couldn't help but laugh. Gracie giggled too. Claire stared at us like we were nuts.

"You sound like the hero in an action movie. No one talks like that."

Claire sucked her cheeks in. Her fingers curled into a fist, and I took a step back.

"Everyone needs to get the hell up right now, or I will throw you to The Licker so I can run away and save myself."

By the tone in her voice, I could tell she meant it.

CHAPTER 15

For the first time maybe ever, River admitted to herself that she'd had too much weed.

After she passed out the circus peanuts, she still had fifteen left in the bag. While they waited for James to turn off the cameras, River snacked. A peanut from the bag, nibbled in six bites. A second, in four bigger bites. Three more ripped in half, each half-eaten one after the other. By the time she got to the last few candies, she had stopped pretending she wasn't going to eat them all. She threw her head back and swallowed the last few whole. The bag was empty before The Licker switched on the lights.

The bright carnival lights paired with the pre-recorded carnival barker's cheers made life unbearable. River, already far too high to handle so much stimulation, ditched Gracie to hide behind a Ms. Pac Man cabinet in the arcade when the screaming started.

She was content to hide behind the cabinet for awhile. The back had a textured panel with edgy little holes that resembled a cheese grater; but the metal felt soft against her skin as she compulsively rubbed it with her palm. She stroked the grate until she had a strange urge to remove the thick layer of dust coating the back of the machine. Black gunk stained her fingers and smudged on her clothes as she rubbed it clean.

Her task was almost complete, and she had hatched a plan to coax herself off the floor when she heard The Licker murder his first victim. At the time, she didn't know it was Lolly, but the terrified wails in the distance made her feel deep in her bones that one of her friends had been killed.

"I'm too high for this," she thought. Her skin turned to rubber; her shoulder blades stretched apart. Her memory flashed a commercial where a grilled cheese got cut in half, and the inside pulled apart all warm and gooey.

"Mmm, grilled cheese," she said to herself. "I should've gotten another one at dinner." Her shoulders stretched as far as her body would allow. She turned into lime flavored seltzer water. Bubbles fizzed on her skin and dissipated in the air.

This stopped when The Licker entered the arcade.

He brandished a baseball bat, and as he walked the aisles of the arcade, he banged the bat side to side, smashing into each game with a metallic thud. River peeked around Ms. Pac Man. She saw his mask and slid further behind the machine.

The Licker didn't seem to notice her. She slowly poked her head back out.

"Smells kinda fishy in here," The Licker said. He laughed, horrible feedback screamed, causing River to shiver. "Salmon swimming upstream? River, get it? Get it? Your vag stinks! No? I can do better. How about this?"

He walked toward the air hockey tables and the skeeball games. He paused next to an air hockey table, raised the bat in the air, and pounded it onto

the thick plastic. It clanged and bounced, but didn't cause any damage. The Licker hit the table again and again, desperate to break it. Each smack of the bat made River flinch; he'd demolish her if he caught her. Still, she couldn't look away.

"They really build these things to last, huh Riv?" he asked. "Guess what? There's more than one way to skin a cat."

The Licker swung the bat into the digital scoreboard mounted above the table. Glass sprayed across the room. He went out of his way to make it crunch under his feet as he stalked the arcade. He jumped the ticket exchange counter to destroy the prize wall. Hats, t-shirts, and other souvenirs were ripped apart and thrown on the floor. Stuffed witches and mummies were beheaded. Plastic pumpkins filled with candy corn were tossed in the air and exploded when they made contact with the bat.

River gently pushed against the game cabinet. It moved a little.

"If he comes over here," she thought. "I'm going to push this thing over on him."

She breathed a sigh of relief. Now she had a plan.

But she didn't need it.

The Licker, bored of wrecking the place, tossed the bat over his shoulder and slunk out the back.

The first time she did edibles, River spent hours binging old Lizzie McGuire episodes. As a result, any time she got too high, a pair of twin alter egos popped in to argue for control over her body. A cliche cartoon angel and devil appeared on each shoulder, drawn in Gracie's signature style. The angel, who she called Harp, was her sober self and served as the voice of reason. The devil, Horn, was a stupid stoner who made her paranoid, lazy, and hungry.

"He's had his fun," said Harp. "He's gone. Stay put. You're in a good spot."

"Your bones are going to disintegrate inside your body," said Horn. "They're buzzing. We gotta go, or the bees are going to get you."

"There aren't any bees," Harp said calmly. "Close your eyes and breathe."

"Why is your mouth so dry? Oh damn, your tongue might be permanently glued to the roof of your mouth," said Horn. "Can you breathe? You can't, can you?"

"Yes, you can breathe," said Harp firmly.

"Nope," said Horn. "If you stay here, you're going to suffocate. You're going to swallow your tongue."

River stuck her tongue out and gently held it between her teeth. She knew she couldn't actually swallow it, but the physical pressure made her feel secure.

"Don't move," ordered Harp. "Don't you dare move."

"Don't listen to her," Horn said. "You're not going to be okay until you get something to drink."

River swallowed, stood, and dusted herself off.

"I tried," mumbled Harp, then she and her evil twin were gone, and River was alone.

There were open doors on either end of the arcade. Since The Licker had gone out the back, River snuck out the front.

A black and blue swirly sign reading MIRROR MAZE hung crookedly above a building forty feet from the arcade. She cracked her back, bent at the waist, and sprinted for the double door entrance. She made it halfway there before someone cut the lights. Her eyes struggled to adjust to the night. She squeezed them shut and rubbed them until the delicate skin threatened to rip. She opened her eyes. She still couldn't see, and the world swirled around her.

Harp gripped her shoulder and whispered "Bathroom" through clenched teeth.

River didn't question the voice and didn't give Horn the chance to rebut. She bolted for the girl's room.

"It's a fridge," said Horn when she opened the door. "People can't hide in fridges. They suffocate. Do not go in there."

A cold breeze from the bathroom stung her lungs. She came back to earth a little, enough to shut up the twins.

Her foot hovered at the threshold, but she couldn't bear to step onto the tile, even though the door had a lock on the inside, and she would be safe. Sandpaper coated her mouth. Her tongue had begun to slide down the back of her throat. Her heart raced and rumbled in her chest.

"There are faucets in the bathroom," she thought. Her mind became consumed with the idea of getting something to drink. Water would make her tongue behave, and then she would stop freaking out. Still, she panicked. There might not be oxygen inside, and the walls could close in and fold over on her at any moment.

She retraced her steps and remembered a food stand advertising "Ghostly Blue Cotton Candy" stationed outside the arcade. Those things always sold bottled water, soda, and juice.

The stand's siren call led her away from the bathroom into a wide, open space with nowhere to hide. In her mind, she bolted from the bathroom at top speed, but in reality, she barely speed walked. The Licker, who saw her from across the park, couldn't believe the luck.

River, too focused on her thirst to feel eyes boring into her skull, didn't notice The Licker walking straight for her.

A little fridge tucked behind the stand held the beverages. She slid the door open and was disappointed to find they were warm. Water seemed like the best option, though she craved lemonade. Unable to decide, she swiped both. The glass lemonade bottle was slightly heavier than the plastic cube holding the water. Her shoulder drooped dramatically on the side carrying the lemonade.

The Licker didn't even bother hiding. River stood right there in the open, bent over to one side, swaying as she ambled toward the Mirror Maze. It would've been funny if River hadn't been so high she could barely walk.

Or maybe that made it funnier.

River chugged half the water. It hit her stomach and caused an immediate wave of nausea. Her chest seized to keep the water down.

Success.

Though she hadn't drunk enough water, she gently placed the bottle at her feet before entering the Mirror Maze. Exhaustion kept her from carrying it any further. She held onto the lemonade because it had become a fifty-pound anchor holding her to the ground.

The Licker entered behind her, keeping a safe distance.

It didn't make sense for River to go inside the Maze when she'd been so scared of the bathroom. The darkness was just as oppressive, and the Maze had narrower walls. At their widest, she could raise her arms to the sides and touch both walls. In the narrowest parts, she had to walk slightly sideways, loudly cursing her father for giving her broad shoulders.

"Horn?" she called out. "Harp? It would be awesome if y'all could tell me what to do now!"

The Licker held back laughter.

Neither twin responded. River was on her own.

Her skin chilled when it grazed the mirrors. She swiped fingers across the glass and allowed them to lead her toward the Maze's center. Her eyes were closed, which probably helped her stay calm.

Behind her, The Licker had trouble keeping it together. River hummed the Winnie the Pooh theme song, first as a slow dirge, then faster and faster until she sounded like a cartoon character riding on a spinning top. When the music got too fast for her mouth, she emitted a shrill screech.

The Licker snapped. River had to die if only to get her to shut the fuck up.

River rounded a corner and opened her eyes. A dim light softly glowed in front of her, with brighter light flashing at the sides. It took a minute before she realized someone was behind her holding a flashlight.

"I'm going to keep walking this way," she said. "If I don't pay attention to you, it takes away your power, and you can't hurt me."

The Licker snorted. "Whatever you say."

Ice shot through her veins at the sound of his altered, demonic voice. She picked up the pace.

The Licker swung the flashlight around above his head. Light reflected off every surface, a swarm of glowing bugs threatened to engulf her. She ducked and ran.

The Licker kept up. He turned the flashlight off. Lucky for him, River wasn't as smart as the others. She didn't think to conceal her deep, fast breaths. No matter which way she turned, her pig-like grunting made her easy to track.

Ahead, River thudded into a wall and screeched. The Licker tiptoed behind her as she regrouped, getting closer and closer until his mask brushed her neck.

River felt the gentle weight of the tongue drop onto her shoulder. She froze.

"Use the bottle as a weapon," she thought, making her first smart decision of the night. She didn't need the twins. She could beat this fucker on her own.

The Licker balanced something on her other shoulder. A button next to her ear clicked, and the mirror in front of her exploded with light. When her eyes adjusted, she stared into his coal-black rubber eyes. The mask's face twisted into a fat, spinning grin.

River elbowed him in the gut. It wasn't much, but it was enough for her break into a sprint. She ping-ponged off the walls, sometimes slamming into dead ends, sometimes making real headway. The Licker stayed at her heels the whole time. He continued to flick the flashlight on and off, which made her head spin.

"Now or never," she said out loud.

She twirled around and went on the offensive. If she put her strength into it, she could hit the creep on the head with the lemonade bottle and seriously injure him. She swatted around until she had a vague idea where his head was, then took a hard swing.

The bottle crashed into a mirror, shattering it.

The Licker cackled.

"Don't laugh! If it can break a mirror, it can break you!" yelled River, genuine fury in her voice.

"Good luck, bitch," he growled.

She swung the bottle again. This time she hit him on his torso. He grunted in amusement. She flailed under him, batting him with the bottle until he grew tired of her attempts.

"Enough!" he said after she whacked what she thought was his ribcage. "You've had your fun."

The Licker shoved her square in the chest on the first try. He turned the flashlight on and dropped it on the ground. A thousand Lickers loomed over a thousand Rivers. Their gray shadows stood in perfect rows over the low light. River turned her head; her doppelgängers turned theirs. She raised and lowered her chin. The other girls did the same. She didn't know where she began and where the reflections ended. Every version of herself gripped the lemonade bottle. Though it wasn't the best weapon in the world, it would do.

The Licker wrapped his fingers in her long hair, which gave her one last rush of energy. She sprang to life. She slammed the bottle into the mirror next to her with all her strength. The bottle didn't break, but the mirror did, revealing a concrete wall. She hit the wall. This time the lemonade bottle exploded. Sticky, sweet smelling liquid gushed in her hand. The bottle slipped. She tightened her fingers, keeping her grip on the neck.

River held the neck and thrust the broken glass at The Licker. She went for the face but missed. Her second swipe made contact. The jagged shards sunk into The Licker's side. He groaned in pain, reached out, and twisted her wrist until the bottle fell to the floor. He pushed River back, and her head slammed into the exposed concrete. Slivers of glass dug into her bare thighs, like ten thousand needles pricking her skin. When she rocked and swayed to stand, the finely ground pieces pierced her and opened holes in her thighs, hands, and knees.

The Licker stood over her, bottle in hand. River raised an arm across her face. Dim rays from the flashlight bounced off the mirrors, doubling and tripling in brightness, allowing her to watch herself be mutilated from every angle.

She closed her eyes.

She didn't want to watch herself die.

He brought the broken bottle down on her head. Bombs burst in her brain. Crunchy, wet squishes echoed in her ears. The Licker breathed loud and hard, muffled by the mask. Her tongue lolled around in her mouth. She bit it weakly, still afraid she might choke.

In the end, he stabbed her twelve times. Three times in the skull, twice in the face, four times in the upper back, once in the lower back, once in the thigh. The last blow went straight into her gut, where he left the bottle deep in her body.

Despite the massive blood loss, it took a few minutes for her to die. As she lay there bleeding out, The Licker picked up the flashlight.

River couldn't move when he knelt over her and shoved his mask in her face. He wrapped gloved fingers around the tongue, and to her surprise, he slid the mask off and held the flashlight under his chin.

No.

Under her chin.

He was a she.

A familiar smile spread across the girl's face, devastating River.

"Why?" she gasped, her last breath imminent.

The Licker laughed. Her real voice was clear and bright without the voice changer. "Does it even matter?" she asked.

"Yes," cried River.

She died before The Licker gave her an answer.

CHAPTER 16

When Claire suggested we hide in the House of Horrors, I laughed so hard Gracie punched me in the arm to shut me up.

"There's a psycho in a cloak and mask chasing us around, and you want to run into a haunted house," I said. "Neither of you can guess the five thousand ways that could go wrong?"

"It's enclosed, and there are plenty hiding places," Claire said. "But that's not why I want to go in. Last summer, I took my little cousin on the ride. It broke. A glow in the dark skeleton dancer guy pulled back a curtain and called someone on a red phone. The ride started again in like thirty seconds."

"Can you make calls outside the park?" I asked.

Claire shrugged. "There's a chance. The phone was in the graveyard. We should get in there before the lights go out again." She paused. All the color drained from her face.

"My immortal soul drifted up," she said. "Just now. It bloomed."

"Oh shit," I mumbled. "Did you get higher?"

"Parts are. My feet are locked. Once again, I find myself tarred and feathered."

Gracie turned to me, mouth open. "We're going to die, aren't we?" she asked.

The facade of Wickett's Despicable House of Horrors was a giant skull. Red eyes bulged from the sockets. Lights inside the eyes pulsed as steam blew from the nose. Jaws stretched wide. Three foot high teeth threatened us as we walked toward the entrance, into the cavernous mouth.

The moment we stepped inside, a growl rolled toward us. Gracie whimpered.

During an ordinary trip through the House, you travel through an old abandoned Victorian, from the swampy front yard to the attic, then your car falls, and you end up in a graveyard. We stood in front of the swamp. Gracie refused to move.

"I'm not going in there," she said.

Claire, whose bones threatened to go full noodle, slung an arm around Gracie's shoulder.

"My four year old cousin giggled her way through this when it was packed with people jumping out to scare us. It's just Halloween decorations, flashing lights, and pre-recorded sounds."

"Smells too," I added. "They pipe in stinky stuff to make it scarier."

We all inhaled.

Fresh dirt. Moldy wood. Sour, acidic vomit.

I gagged.

"Puking is bad," said Claire. "No!" She swatted at my face, missed, and patted me on the head.

"Are you aware I'm not a dog?" I asked.

Gracie ignored me and twisted toward Claire. "Did you put your arm around me to guide me into the building, or did you do it so I could hold you?"

"Yes," said Claire. Her eyes drifted in opposite directions. "Maybe I ate too much weed."

"Trust me," I said. "You did."

While Gracie dragged Claire into the House, I did some mental math.

Gracie was the shyest person I'd ever met and just as much of a stoner as River. While River used weed to calm her anxiety, Gracie used it to bring herself out of her shell. Being high didn't make her fearless or anything, but it did help her behave like a normal human who could have a conversation with strangers without crying.

I didn't know how much THC Gracie would need to consume to muster up the guts to survive the night. However, I had a sneaking suspicion she hadn't eaten enough. With Claire practically down for the count, our survival might rely on me.

Metallic fake blood stench hung in the air, and dinner churned in my stomach.

"We have to go," I said as calmly as possible. "Let's follow the tracks. Move as fast as you can while we still have light."

I ducked under Claire's other arm. Her skin was damp; her hair smelled like coconut. Heat radiated from her core. Her chin fell to her chest; her head rolled toward me.

"I love you, Violet," she said. "Mean it. Do you love me?"

"Yes," I said, my dry lips sticking together as I spoke.

"If we don't die, you wanna get married?"

I sighed. We didn't have time for a drugged out love fest. My high had worn off, replaced by sweaty drowsiness.

"Sure," I said to quiet her.

"I love you too, Gracie."

"Yeah, Claire, everybody loves everyone," grunted Gracie. She pointed to a dark corner. "Can we cut through those curtains over there to get to the graveyard?"

We dragged Claire through the fake swamp. A cigarette butt and Starburst wrapper floated in the green-tinged water. Plastic reeds slapped our calves. Claire stepped a little too hard and splashed herself in the face.

Gracie gave me full control of Claire while she peeked through a curtain.

"This is the haunted dining room," she said.

I tried to imagine the ride layout.

James had a friend who ran the Black Kitten Coaster, and he got us passes on a super slow weekend one sweltering July. I thought the House was stupid. Plastic skeletons, dusty walls, and dirty standing water aren't scary, even if you dress them up with strobe lights and smoke effects. I protested until James reminded me they keep it extra cold inside, and we could sit in the little coffin-shaped cars to cool off. We went through the House seven or eight times, more than enough to memorize the layout.

"If we go to the dining room, we can turn right and go through the attic. The graveyard is right after," I said.

We pulled Claire through the curtain. She immediately broke free to sit on a creaky wooden dining chair. I held my breath, preparing for it to disintegrate under her. It swayed a little but remained intact.

"Whoever decorated this place did a great job," Claire said. She rubbed her finger in a circle on the table and drew a Ghostbusters slash across the center.

She wasn't wrong.

From the blood-stained damask rug on the floor to the water stains on the walls, to the too realistic roasted pig on the table, the details were impeccable.

I leaned in to check out poor Porky. Fake flies dotted the rotten apple in his mouth.

"No time to sit," I said. "We're super close."

"Leave me," said Claire. "Slowin' ya down."

Something inside me snapped.

"Can I ask what part of 'no one is splitting up' did y'all not understand?" I yelled. "Claire, snap out of it. When you slept over after Avery Eaton dumped you, I watched you take two 250 milligram brownies, spread Nutella on them to make a sandwich, and eat it in three bites. Four hours later, you helped my mom mount our new kitchen cabinets. Tonight you had a fraction of that amount. You can walk. Now take a big breath, stand straight, and walk behind me. Gracie, you take the rear."

Claire shivered, gripping the table. She did a full body roll with her eyes closed. Gracie's brow furrowed.

"Claire," she began.

"Wait," I mouthed to her, holding up a hand.

Claire shook, tapped her fingers on the table, and hummed *The Yellow Rose of Texas* at half speed. I'd seen her do this before hitting the pool at a meet. Her coach taught it to the swim team as a grounding exercise. I didn't understand it, but they were the number one team in their division, so it must have had some value. After the first chorus, Claire stopped and sat mannequin still, then did another body roll out of the chair, kicking it over behind her.

"Violet, ho!" she cheered, clapping a hand on my right shoulder. Gracie placed a shaky hand on Claire's shoulder. We were a real human centipede.

The attic was built on an incline that slightly tilted to the right. Strobe lights beat faster and faster, causing my pulse to race. Stacks of old televisions - the boxy kind my Grandma had in her guest room - flashed static as crunching white noise played from the cheap, tinny speakers. Hands hit the windows, and hungry zombies climbed the house trying to break in. A pre-recorded orchestra played a mediocre version of *Don't Fear the Reaper*.

When the ride is active, zombies break through and lurch toward your car. They get as close to your coffin as the rules allowed, clawing at the air, miming your dismemberment.

That night only the strobes, televisions, and orchestra greeted us. Even without the zombies, the room gave me the creeps.

"The exit is through the bookcase," I said. "It splits in the middle."

We pushed the doors open and stared into a black hallway.

"There's a drop, right?" asked Claire.

"Yeah," I said. "I wonder if there are stairs hidden somewhere."

"We can climb in," said Gracie.

I shook my head. "It's too dark. Anything could be hiding in the dark."

Claire squatted, turned, and lowered a leg into the darkness. Her foot softly thudded against the ground.

"It's not steep," she said. "It's not flat either. We have to crawl. Once you're in here, there's gray light at the end. Those strobes are giving me a headache, and I might lose my shit again. If you want me to stay coherent, y'all gotta hustle."

Without fanfare, Claire climbed into the opening and parkoured her way down the drop.

"Who wants to go first?" I asked Gracie.

She squinted into the darkness. "It's wide enough for us to go side by side."

We crawled backward on our knees. Damp concrete scuffed my hands while the cold metal track pressed against my belly. I breathed a sigh of relief when the ground leveled enough for us to walk.

Fog floated to our knees, intensified by pale, static blue light. Tall, fake headstones in crooked rows with names like "Anita Moore-Tishan" and "Rustin Peece" made good hiding places for actors dressed as ghosts. They'd jump out and scream, inches from your face. Though I knew the room was empty, I braced myself for a jump scare.

Claire and Gracie walked the rows while I climbed over a dead tree to reach the phone.

My hand gripped the thin curtain. I said a quick prayer and pulled it to reveal the red phone.

"Found it!" I called out.

I swallowed a cry and lifted the receiver. There were no buttons on the phone. It must've rung directly to another line. I pressed the phone to my ear, praying it might somehow dial 911.

A tone chirped in my ear, followed by a bubbly ring.

Riiiiiing.

Riiiiiing.

Riiiiiing.

"Hello?" A robotic voice growled. "You've reached customer service."

I slammed the phone back on the receiver.

"What's going on?" asked Gracie.

"He answered," I said.

"Who?"

"Him."

Grace placed a hand on her throat. "Does that mean he's in here with us?"

Somewhere in the background, Claire quietly called out to us. "Y'all?"

"I don't know," I said, ignoring Claire. "The line could connect to the security office or a control room or some random phone across the park or pretty much anywhere."

"What do we do?" asked Gracie.

"Y'all?" Claire repeated.

Gracie panicked, pacing and wringing her hands. I ignored her.

"What Claire?" I asked.

"Can you come here? I'm so high I'm hallucinating. Or I hope I am."

Claire stood over four gravestones. Someone had turned them around and carved new names on the reverse side.

LOLLY BISHOP

MILA KELLEY

RIVER ELLIS

THEODORE GORDON

"What does this mean?" I asked. The room swirled around me. Blue light illuminated Claire, lighting her hair like a halo around her head. Her lower lip quivered. She took my hand, lacing her fingers through mine.

"What does what mean?" asked Gracie.

"The names on the gravestones," I said.

"If Lolly is dead," Claire whispered. "Are Mila and River too?" Her chest twitched, she gasped for air. She groaned into my shoulder as I wrapped her in a hug. Tears and snot soaked my shoulder.

"Something might have happened to the others," I said. "Or maybe not. Maybe this is The Licker's wish list and he hasn't gotten to some of them yet."

Gracie walked behind me. She read the gravestones, silently mouthing each name. She stopped at River.

"River's dead," she said, a whisper of a whisper.

"Don't say that," I said, reaching out to her. She slid away.

"River's dead," Gracie repeated, louder and faster, her words filled with alarm.

"Gracie, he could be in here listening to us. Do not freak out. You're jumping to conclusions."

"Why's her name on a gravestone, Violet? Why her and Lolly and Mila and not us?"

Claire pulled away from me. She sniffed. "Maybe ours are over there," she said.

"No," Gracie said. "River is dead. What. What do I do? I can't be a person without her. We're supposed to be writing a book. We were going to do a tour next year. We were going to rent a house in Austin and get nerdy boyfriends and a cat. We were going to name it Raccoon."

I flashed back to the day a literary agent sent a direct message to the social media account where River and Gracie posted their daily comics. River cried, and Gracie skipped through the halls at school singing, uncharacteristic behaviors for each of them. The agent said *Graceful River* was hilarious and could be a book, merch, maybe even a TV series. Neither girl could stop smiling. They started the comic as a way to spend more time together, not for fame. Gracie's parents found River suspicious, but as long as the girls spent time creating art, Mr. and Mrs. Scott figured they couldn't get into too much trouble. They didn't know the girls got high when they worked. Edibles were the secret sauce behind the success.

"Gracie," I said. "This doesn't mean River is dead."

Gracie stood and kicked River's gravestone over. She fell to her knees and beat it with both fists until her hands bled. Claire bent over to restrain her.

"Don't you fucking talk to me!" she screamed. "What if it was James?"

My heart stopped. In all the panic, I hadn't even thought about James.

But if her name wasn't on gravestone...

"We don't know what the names mean," I said.

"Yes," said Gracie. "We do."

"If they're dead, where the fuck are the bodies?" asked Claire.

Gracie wailed.

I knelt next to Gracie.

"If something happened to River or James, there's nothing we can do right now. We need to keep moving, and we need to have a plan. Now let's think. Who is Theodore Gordon?" I asked. "Is he from Pritchett?"

"I have a neighbor named Mr. Gordon across the street," said Claire. "I can't remember his first name. He works at night. I don't see him much."

I slowly turned my head toward her. "Works at night where?"

Claire swallowed.

Tiny words were written above and below his name. I leaned

in to read them. Above Theodore, it read, "Here Lies." Below his name, they'd scratched the words, "His head."

My foot brushed against something in the fog. Soft, firm, heavy. I gently kicked it.

"I really hope this is a soccer ball," I said.

I fanned at the fog. Blue light reflected off something at my feet.

Glasses.

On a head.

On a *severed* head.

I screamed and ran. Red, orange, and yellow plastic strips flew in the air around the exit. The words **WELCOME TO HELL** screamed from above a bleeding arch. I ran through and burst free from the House of Horrors.

My body hit another, knocking us both to the ground. I crawled away, flopping back and forth like a fish.

"Wait," said a little voice. "I found you. I found you."

Blythe sat sprawled on the ground with blood smeared on her clothes. She smiled. Her teeth were streaked with red.

"I found you," she said again. "We are found."

CHAPTER 17

Claire and Gracie appeared behind Blythe.

"What happened to you?" Gracie gasped.

Blythe laid down on the ground and made a low bun out of her hair so she could use it as a pillow.

"I have to sleep," she said. "I'm *soooooo* sleepy."

"She's more baked than me," Claire said, laughing.

"She's not even a person anymore," I said.

Gracie hovered over Blythe. "Where is the blood coming from?"

Blythe didn't react when I lifted her leg to examine the deep cut on her calf, or when I lifted her shirt to check for bruises on her stomach. Her fingers were raw, her gel nails torn off, her real nails ripped down to nubs. More bruises encircled a small, bloody gash on her forehead.

I gently slapped her cheek.

"Blythe, what happened?"

Blythe took the end of my ponytail and twirled it around her fingers.

"No paper towels in the bathroom," she said. "Couldn't dry my hands. I thought there might be some at a drink cart outside. I lost you. Stuff happened. A hurricane went through the midway. I got scared and hid. I heard him hurt Mila. She made the worst sounds. Screaming, then gurgling, then nothing. Then he found me. The gross tongue mask from before."

"You saw him?" I asked.

"Telling you duh, bitch," Blythe said. She pushed herself up on her elbows. "He had, um, something heavy. I saw it, and he dropped it and chased me. He dragged me through the Black Kitten Coaster by my leg on my face. Couldn't feel anything. Numb. Something happened, and he left me. I think he thought I was dead. He went away. I stayed a long time, then I left. Hid behind a trash can, then a picnic table. Saw a huge blood trail outside the Mirror Maze. Saw tongues coming back to the Black Kitten Coaster for me. Ran. Fell a couple times. Found you."

"You're sure it was blood outside the Mirror Maze?" I asked.

Blythe wrapped my hair around my neck like a noose and pulled me close, choking me.

"When you see blood, you know blood, you *feel* blood," she said through gritted teeth, laughing maniacally.

"So…Blythe's gone," Claire laughed.

I freed my hair from Blythe's grip and sat back.

"What do we do?" I asked.

Blythe was way too out of it to walk around, especially when Claire was threatening to drift off again and couldn't help wrangle her. A thousand scenarios ran through my head.

Hide. *Then what? The new security guard won't be here until morning. That's plenty of time to find us.*

Security booth. *What if The Licker is holed up there? That could've been where he picked up the phone.*

Climb the gate. *Those spikes at the top are too sharp. Mila cut her shoe, I'd probably cut my throat, if I could even climb it in the first place.*

Get back to the door where we broke in. *Maybe the best option, but again, we can't carry Blythe and stay hidden.*

"He could be anywhere," I said. "Blythe, if we hide you, will you stay put?"

"No promises," she said, a sly grin on her face.

I snapped my fingers in her face. "I'm serious. This is life or death. All you have to do is curl up like a kitty and fall asleep. We will get help and come get you."

"I'm *soooooo* sleepy," Blythe reminded us.

"Where do you want to put her?" Gracie asked me.

"The last car on the House of Horrors train. It's a working coffin. Someone hides in it and pops out when you're in the graveyard. We'll stick her in there and close the lid."

"We're putting people in coffins?" Gracie asked. "Is this really happening? Like, for real?"

"You're coffining me?" Blythe asked.

I rubbed my temples. "We're not burying you or anything. Pretend it's a tanning bed. You like those."

Ever the drama queen, Blythe flopped back on the ground and went limp.

Claire threw Blythe over her shoulder and carried her around the House back into the entrance. She laid her neatly in the coffin and closed the lid.

Blythe cried out when it clicked shut.

"You're fine," I said. "Safer than the rest of us."

"Meow," she said, her voice muffled. "Purr, purr, meow. Night!"

"What the hell?" I asked.

"You told her to act like a kitty and fall asleep," Gracie told me. "It's your fault."

Claire, Gracie, and I waited. When Blythe remained quiet for a few minutes, Claire dug around at the employee stand at the House entrance, and I led Gracie away to explain my plan.

"We have to help Blythe and anyone else who might still be alive out there," I said. "We're going to head to the front. If the security office is empty, we're calling 911, and then we're escaping through the gate and running until we either get help or die of natural causes. Got it?"

"What if we stayed in the office and locked ourselves in?" Gracie asked.

"Don't you think he could break through the glass?"

"I don't know," she said. "I'm not a fast runner. I've got asthma."

"Asthma, or death by carousel?" I asked.

"How do you kill someone with a carousel?"

I held my index fingers up by my temples to mimic horns. "The devils have horns," I said. "Impale someone through the heart."

Gracie raised her eyebrows and gave me a once over.

"Violet," she said, leaning in close. "You can tell me. Are you the killer?"

I paused. "Yes. I'm the killer, and I'm going to murder you at the fortune teller booth when I beat your head in with her crystal ball."

"Graphic."

"It's been one helluva night," I said.

Claire came to us, bearing gifts. A hammer for me, a matte black metal flashlight for Gracie.

"There aren't any batteries in the flashlight," Claire said. "It's heavy enough to hurt someone if you swing it hard enough. Hammer is self-explanatory. I have this."

She lifted an electric drill and pulled the trigger twice. It buzzed with promise. Claire wiggled her eyebrows in excitement.

"Maybe Claire's the killer," Gracie said under her breath.

"Gals, what's the plan?" Claire asked.

I laid it out for her. She agreed with Gracie and wanted to barricade ourselves in the office.

"Violet, I swear those windows aren't even glass," she said. "They're some kind of plastic. This guy practically teleports, and if you and Gracie can't run fast enough…"

"I can run fast," I protested.

"You joined the marching band to get a P.E. credit because you didn't want to run the mile, and you don't even play a band instrument. No one marches with a violin."

"I carry the flag," I said.

"They bought a lighter flag because you couldn't lift the original pole."

"Point taken."

A crack echoed through the carnival as the lights cut out. The rides droned as they wound down, then went silent.

Gracie instinctively tried to turn on the flashlight.

"I told you there aren't any batteries," Claire whispered.

Gracie shook the flashlight aggressively. "Just checking."

The quieter I tried to make my steps, the louder they became, so I gave up and walked like a normal person. Claire and Gracie were close behind me, and I was only mildly worried Claire might slip and accidentally drill one of us.

When we made it to the midway, something swished past us. I caught a glimpse of The Licker's flowing cloak. He didn't pursue us, but he was too close for comfort.

Claire, ever the hero, corralled us into the midway. Gracie and I hid in the kissing booth while Claire held watch. Footsteps pounded the ground, louder and louder, stopped, and ran away.

Claire knelt. "He ran toward the carousel," she said.

"See. Carousel as murder weapon," I told Gracie. I turned to Claire. "This means if we go to the security booth, he'll see us."

"Not necessarily," Gracie said. "He could be doing a sweep. The carousel is past security. If we cut around to the left, we can cling to the gate and go around that way. It's longer, we'll be out of his reach. For a minute, anyway."

"Or," said Claire, standing tall and brandishing her drill. "We know where he's going, so we follow him and end this." She revved the drill.

"Do you have a death wish?" I asked. "Because I sure don't."

"Us three can overpower him," she said. "Blythe managed to survive."

"Because she is so high, he thought she was dead!"

Gracie leaned close to me. "I mean, that plan might work. Claire can kick a grown man's ass. She can pin him while we bash his brains in. But I don't know if it will work if the lights aren't on."

"Since they're *not* on, what's your plan?" I asked.

"Gate. Security. Hide."

Claire protested until she realized she'd been overruled.

I led them down the alley behind the midway, past the bathrooms, behind a trio of yellow leaved trees. As we rounded the corner, the lights came back on.

The Licker stood twelve feet away, staring directly at the trees.

"Aren't you dumbasses supposed to be hiding from me?" he asked.

"Run!" yelled Gracie. She turned to getaway.

Claire grabbed her.

"Yeah," Claire said. "Run toward *him!*"

Claire burst through the trees, drill high over her head. The Licker reached into his deep pocket and pulled out a hunting knife as long as my arm. He stomped toward Claire, ready to slice and dice.

"Come on," I told Gracie, holding out my hand. To my surprise, she took it.

Claire and The Licker collided in front of us. Claire smashed him with her shoulder and elbowed him in the stomach, dropping him to the ground with a thud. She pinned him and tried to pry the knife from his hand. He held on for dear life. He shook his head back and forth violently, slapping her in the face with his stupid tongue. Claire bit his shoulder. Her teeth left two small holes in his cloak. The Licker let out a robotic yelp, which scared Claire enough that he managed to wriggle from her grasp.

"Hit me!" he said, laughing gleefully.

I'd never been in a fight before. Once I jumped in, I don't remember exactly what I did, what Claire did, or even what The Licker did. Bodies rolled in the dirt; weapons flew through the air. A fist hit his face. The flashlight slammed into the ground. My hammer crushed The Licker's empty hand.

I didn't just want this guy dead. I wanted him unmasked. I dropped my hammer and fought to get my fingers under the rubber neck. His huge glove wrapped around my hand and squeezed until something popped. I twisted my wrist to freedom.

Gracie and I managed to pin his arms to his sides. We held him while the drill purred. Claire leaned in, ready to jam the bit straight into his chest.

Unfortunately, her aim was off, and she slid it into my arm instead. I yelped, falling backward. The Licker pushed Gracie aside and scrambled away. Claire dropped the drill and checked my arm.

"Grazed the skin. Didn't go through. You're fine, you're fine. Keep moving."

Gracie shrieked. The Licker was on his feet.

Claire's drill was in his hand.

He revved it while pulling his tongue taught with his other hand. He held the bit to the back of his tongue and drilled up through the rubber. He laughed into his voice changer.

"Thanks for the gift," he said.

I bolted, with Claire slightly ahead and Gracie at my heels, struggling to breathe.

I screamed for Claire to turn around and run for the security booth. She either didn't hear me or didn't want to listen, because she ran into the midway. Gracie crashed against my back.

"Listen," she gasped. "The hissing. It's his breathing!"

A rhythmic, whistling wheeze approached.

"Why aren't we moving?" I asked.

"Go, go, go! Follow Claire!"

Gracie dug her fingers into my side and, before I could protest, pushed me into the midway.

CHAPTER 18

Next to the Ferris wheel and the Whirling Witch Coaster, the midway was always my least favorite part of the carnival. I hated the rides because I thought I might end up dead if I rode them. I hated the midway because it was filthy.

Whoever cleaned the carnival skipped the narrow, sharp rows. Shredded napkins and wrappers littered the ground. Years old water stains crept up the fabric dividers between booths. Dusty plywood walls with sharp splinters stood ready to rip your clothes. The men and women running the booths weren't required to be friendly like the ride operators and ticket takers. Instead of neatly branded Poison Apple Halloween Carnival uniforms, they wore sweat-stained t-shirts and ugly baseball caps with crooked, peeling "Carnival midway" logos emblazoned on the front. You'd give them a token, and you'd get a chance to toss a bean bag or fire an ancient pop gun. If you lost their game, they'd grunt and demand a token to pay for another round. If you won, they'd chuck a cheap prize at your chest.

The worst ones were dirty old men who asked our ages and grumbled slurs under their breath when we said seventeen.

"He likes them young," River told me once after the man at

the ring toss booth called us sluts. "A few years ago I told him I was fourteen, and he told me how pretty I was and tried to give me a stuffed heart. I guess since I got my license I'm not the freshest produce anymore."

Thoughts about River twisted like a knife in my ribs.

"I'm gonna hurl," Gracie groaned. "It smells like lemon, cheese, and metal in here."

I nodded. A stink tornado from a dozen Paulie's Pop-A-Corn carts popping a dozen different flavors choked us. I loved their salted birthday cake flavor, but I didn't love it mixed with the pickle relish flavor, and I *despised* it mixed with the scent of blood.

I wrapped an arm around her and pulled her behind a face painting booth. We waited for The Licker to pop up and attack us. When he didn't, I fell to the ground and crawled under a stool. Gracie joined me.

"My eyes hurt," I told her. "There's sweat in them."

She offered me a white cocktail napkin emblazoned with a gold Jinkx Room logo. I mopped my brow and asked if she wanted it back.

"Gross," she said. "Keep it. Keep this too." She handed me a hammer.

"Where did you find this?" I asked.

"I picked it up when we ran. Did we learn our lesson about dropping our weapons in front of a murderer?"

"Yes," I said. "We did."

"Good. Now what?"

I surveyed the area. We were by a little booth where you could throw ping pong balls into goldfish bowls to win a live goldfish. Rusted shelves displaying glass spheres lined the walls. Black and orange fish delicately swam inside their tiny, solitary prisons, except for one who floated limply at the top of his bowl.

I tapped the glass, and the water rippled. The dead fish's eye squished against the bowl. I leaned in for a better look, and movement in the reflection made me spin around, my hands squeezed into fists, ready to fight.

No one was there.

"I'm so tired," I told Gracie. I relaxed my hands. The adrenaline fueling my survival instinct had drained. "I'm light-headed. I can't do this much longer."

"We'll do it as long as we have to," she said. "He's in here somewhere. We have to keep running, or we have to find a better hiding place. We also have to be prepared to fight." She sneered, cracked her neck, and spit on the ground.

Gracie was possibly the calmest, most even keeled person I'd ever met. When in a group of more than three people, she rarely spoke at all. She would sit in the corner and let everyone chatter like chickens while she doodled little pictures in her pink and white checkered sketchbook. I'd forget she was there until I checked *Graceful River's* social media the next day to find our conversations reenacted by Gracie's squatty faced, bug-eyed characters.

"Since when did you become a badass?" I asked, nodding at the spit puddle on the ground.

"He killed my best friend. If I get my chance, I'm going to make him pay."

The phrase "best friend" made my heart skip. James had disappeared into the carnival earlier that evening, and she could've been anywhere. I reminded myself that her name hadn't been on a tombstone, as though that guaranteed her safety.

"He's going to pay," I assured her. "For River and whoever else he hurts. He's going to rot in jail."

"I don't want him to go to jail. I want him dead. If I see him again, I'm going to take your hammer and bash his brains in. I wish I'd drilled a hole in his head when I had the chance. You said he crushed Lolly's head? I want to crush all the bones in his body. I want to taste his blood."

My eyes bulged. "Let's not get too upset yet," I told her. "Emotions breed mistakes. We need to keep it together."

In the distance, a siren blared, followed by childish giggles. A

Choo Choo Train whistle tooted. Someone had turned on the Black Kitten Coaster.

"There are eyes on us," said Gracie. "It's like there's a million spiders running down my neck. When I turn my head, I expect his nasty ass tongue to flop in my face."

The same paranoia plagued me. The whole situation felt like a setup, like my friends and I were pawns in a gory chess game. He messed with the rides and lights to disorient us, kept us apart to torture us. He probably wanted us in the midway, trapped in our own little fishbowl, laying in wait until he won the game and could claim us as his prize.

"Are you still high?" I asked.

"I can function. When the lights are on, they're super bright, and when it's dark, everything is extra black. Sounds are intense. If the stupid coaster doesn't stop laughing, I will tear my hair out and shove it in my ears. I'm overstimulated, not loopy or anything."

"I'm worried about Claire," I said. "She couldn't even speak proper English."

"Blythe was worse. Bitch couldn't stay on her feet."

"She's safe in her coffin, though. Claire's in the wild."

I picked at the rubber rim on my shoe until a strip peeled off like a banana skin. I stretched it between my fingers until it snapped.

"Should we try to find her?" I asked.

"We should *think*. Use our brains. Let's make a list."

Gracie pulled her sketchbook and a ballpoint pen from her crossbody bag. Thick, block letters on the pen spelled out GOODE BOOKS. She'd swiped it from her publisher's office when she and River signed their publishing deal.

She made two columns, one a list of our names, the other a list of locations.

LOLLY – TEST YOUR STRENGTH
RIVER – ?
MILA – ?
CLAIRE – MIDWAY
BLYTHE – HOH
VIOLET – MIDWAY
JAMES – ?
GRACIE – MIDWAY

"What are you trying to figure out?" I asked.

"Lolly is dead. It's likely Mila and River are too," she said. "We need to rule them out. Blythe is hidden. I have faith she will stay put."

"I don't."

She sighed. "Neither do I, but I have to hope. Claire is somewhere near us. I can sense her out there, alive. You and I are okay. James is the only one left."

Gracie added a few more question marks next to James' name.

"What if Lolly wasn't the first victim?" I asked. "What if he got James before her?"

"No. Stop imagining the worst, think critically. When would he have had time to kill James? Didn't he pretty much move straight for Lolly after the lights came on?"

"What if he snatched James in the dark?"

"There is no way someone put their hands on James Parker without her screaming bloody murder."

"What if he surprised her?"

Gracie drew a circle, then two more, to make eyes on a face. She drew little Xs for pupils. The mouth was a straight line with a little half-moon tongue hanging limply from one side. She sighed. "I'd believe James was the psycho in the costume before I'd believe The Licker killed her without an earthshaking fight." She drew a second face, this one with sharp fangs and cat eyes.

I ripped the pen from her hand.

"Don't joke about James hurting people. She would never."

"I was being flippant. I'm sorry. James is fine. There's a nonzero chance she escaped to get help. The police might roll in here any minute with James perched on the hood of a cop car, pointing the way like George Washington Crossing the Delaware."

We sat in silence. Gracie traced a blank page with a finger. I returned her pen.

"What do we do with your list?" I asked.

"I don't know," she said. "I thought if I wrote a list on paper, I'd magically have a plan. I don't. I can write names all day long, and it won't change anything. James and Claire are missing. Blythe is barely human. Everyone else is dead. We're on our own."

"Do you want to try to find Claire?"

Gracie's face cracked. "Am I a horrible person if I say no? I'm scared, Violet. This doesn't feel like reality. Is it? Is this really happening?"

My head throbbed. Her inability to process the situation irritated me, but if any situation warranted grace, this was it.

"It's happening," I said softly.

"I love Claire. I love all our friends. But I don't want to die here. I want to save myself."

"Then that's what we're going to do," I said, gripping my hammer. "If we go straight and kinda follow the turns without changing direction, we can go behind the face painting stations and turn right at the end by Madame Lavona. From there, it's a straight shot down balloon game alley, and we exit at the dunk tank. Once we escape, we'll get help to save the others."

"Is this really happening?" she repeated.

"Yeah. It is."

"And Claire?"

I swallowed. "It's like you said. We have to save ourselves. We aren't acting selfish. Claire's stronger than us. She's fine."

CHAPTER 19

C laire wasn't fine.

Though she'd successfully managed to escape The Licker upon entering the midway, she'd hit her head during their earlier scuffle, and he'd crushed her arm under his foot before twisting it behind her back. Fortunately she'd been able to scramble away, but he'd left her with enough injuries that she'd have gone into shock if she hadn't eaten River's edibles.

Her right temple throbbed. One of her back molars wiggled when she poked it with her tongue. Her left arm was at least sprained, probably broken. The fingers on her right hand were definitely broken. Tears welled in her eyes when she pictured Hattie Bakely pitching softball in her place.

She doubled back to the entrance and stepped into the open area by the carousel. In the distance, the fat pumpkin on the Ferris Wheel grinned at her, flashing his broken teeth as a sign of solidarity.

"I'm smashed up too," he said. "Won't be stopping me."

Claire's skin crawled. Overwhelmed by the pumpkin's gaze, she stumbled away and hid in the shadowy space between the midway and the gate. Dumpsters lined the row, and Claire thought it must be awful to be an employee who had to walk the alley in the summer, inhaling the stink of lawn trimmings, empty plastic bags coated with slimy snow cone syrup, and wet cardboard boxes. She sniffed her armpits. It smelled like she'd used a Whataburger with extra onions as deodorant. The dumpsters had nothing on her.

For awhile she could still hear Violet and Gracie. Hard breathing, squeals, shushes. They were still on the move. Their voices grew faint as they headed deeper into the midway. Claire strained to listen. Crunchy dirt beneath her feet Velcroed her to the earth as an invisible anchor attached to her spine held her core in place. She had major couch lock, and she wasn't even on a couch.

She'd suffered from sleep paralysis off and on for years. She would wake in the darkness, her mind firing on all cylinders, her body refusing to cooperate. Over time she learned that if she could move one pinky, one toe, or even wiggle her nose, it would send an energy rush over her body and propel her from sleep. She grunted as she slid one foot an inch across the concrete. A single step would get her legs moving and break her out of her weird fear-driven stoner haze.

"You have to move," she told her feet. "He knows where you are. He knows you're alone. Your feet are fine. You can run. One in front of the other." She pushed her foot a little further, then further still, until her legs threatened to send her to the ground in a wide split. She fell, but she caught herself and stumbled into a trot.

There was no way she'd be able to scale the daggered gate with her injured hand. She would have to get back to the employee entrance and walk out. No, run out.

"Stay in the dark," she told herself. "Get to the phone. Call someone. Save the other girls. Get home alive. Stay in the dark. Get to a phone. Get across the parking lot. Get to a car. Get to a neighborhood. No one can outrun you. You're the fastest girl in school."

Claire picked up the pace, but the speed and heat and bright lights messed with her head, sickening her. She doubled over, took a few deep breaths, and switched to power walking. Even at a slower speed, Claire was still faster than most. She pictured spectators in the stands at a swim meet, all chanting her name. She got carried away and chanted it herself.

"Go Claire, go!" she cheered. She might as well have blown an air horn to give away her location.

The cheers in her head faded into laughter as she sensed someone looming behind her.

She stopped.

"Whatcha doing, Claire?" an amused, radio static filtered voice asked.

The Licker knew her name.

He gripped the drill in his gloved hand, pressing the trigger to show it still held a charge. Her heart hummed in time with the sound.

"No," Claire said. "This isn't happening."

"Rah rah, go, Claire, go!" he teased. "Oh. Speaking of 'rah rah,' you shouldn't expect Mila to pop out with her pom-poms. It's hard to cheer with a water gun jammed down your throat."

"What did you do to her?"

"I had to crack her jaw in half to get it in. All that money her parents spent on veneers, wasted."

His words took Claire's breath away.

Little Mila, her strong voice and pretty face, was gone. They hadn't had a chance to say goodbye. Not to Claire, not to anyone. Her parents adored her. They went to every single game and cheer competition to cheer their cheerleader. For events, cheer parents wore t-shirts with their child's face hand-painted on the front and their graduation year and squad position on the back. Claire was at Mila's house when her mom's shirt for Senior year came in the mail. She actually squealed when she unfolded it. Mila's cartoony face on one side, bold letters proclaiming the wearer to be the cheer captain's mom on the other. She put it on over her clothes and wore it out to dinner, even though Mila begged her not to. Mrs. Kelly's daughter had worked her ass off for almost a decade so her mother could wear it, and she intended to milk it for all it was worth.

Claire pictured Mila's mother standing over a casket wearing the shirt.

Her body tensed as she prepared to run, dizziness be damned.

"If you run, I'll catch you," he told her. "Don't run. I'm not moving, don't you move either. Turn around and look at me. It's hard to hear anything inside this mask."

"Maybe you should take it off," Claire yelled over her shoulder.

"Or maybe I should take your fucking head off with this drill," he countered.

Terrified, Claire gave in and turned around. The Licker kept his promise; he didn't move.

"I'm curious, Claire, have you wondered why I'm doing this? What's my motivation? If I were in your shoes, I'd have so many questions."

"There's never a good reason to murder people. You're crazy."

"False," he said. "Tell me, Claire. What are your plans for tomorrow?"

"What?"

"What are you going to do tomorrow," he repeated, mocking her tone. He buzzed the drill on and off in his hand, taunting her more than words ever could.

She pictured her pool. Her parents built for her to practice at home, her cool blue haven. She could stick her earbuds in and crank her music, dive in, and glide through the water for hours. Sometimes she only stopped when the music died.

"I'm going to breakfast with the girls at the Crave Inn," she said. "I'll shower and sleep after, then I'll swim."

"You swim every day?"

"Yes."

"To keep in shape for racing?"

"No," she said, shaking her head. "I swim because I love swimming."

"See," he said. He tucked the drill under his arm and clapped his hands. "Right there. I don't love anything. I don't even like anything."

"Do you especially not like us? Me and my friends? What did we do to you?"

The Licker took a step forward. He pointed the business end of the drill directly at her face as he made the bit spin. Claire clenched her jaw until her gums bled. Electricity shot through her back teeth. She sharply sucked on her teeth. Her mouth tasted like pennies. She snorted and spat in his direction.

"It's not about not liking you," he said, dodging the flying spit. "I don't particularly dislike any of you. Well, James I can take or leave." He cackled. "Maybe I'll take her and leave her in chunks." He leaned close to her and growled. "Maybe I already have."

She ignored his threat against James. She couldn't handle more than one dead friend at a time.

"So we know you?" she asked.

"As much as anyone can know anyone else."

Claire put her hands in the air in surrender.

"Take off your mask," she said. "If you're going to kill me anyway, you might as well tell me who you are. It's only fair."

"Do you think I'm stupid?"

"Kinda," Claire said, smirking.

The drill stopped.

"You have some nerve," he said.

"You don't. If you did, you wouldn't be wearing your nasty mask."

He took another step toward her.

"I'm not taking off the fucking mask. I might take yours off, though."

He crashed his body into hers and wrapped his biceps around her waist, pinning her injured arm behind her back. Her screams overpowered the evil canned laughter at the House of Horrors. He pressed the drill bit into her cheek and hit the trigger.

The drill cut into her cheek at an angle, ripping the flesh apart and cracking her bottom teeth into dust. Blood filled her mouth and rushed down her throat, choking her. The pain burned white until she didn't feel anything at all. He chucked the drill, stuck a leather-clad finger into the hole in her face, and then tore off her entire cheek.

He thrust the shred of skin down the front of her shirt, into her bra. "Safe keeping," he hissed.

She cried, begging with words neither he nor she could understand. Without her teeth and cheek, her tongue flopped out of her mouth, mirroring The Licker's mask.

Claire fought weakly as he dragged her into the alley behind the midway. When her blood made her arms too slick to grip, he reached under his cloak and pulled out a belt.

He kneed her in the chest and dropped her at his feet. She tried to crawl away. He tsk-tsked her and wrapped her hair around his fingers, pulling her back. He looped the belt around her neck and used it as a leash to lead her to the food court. She clawed at the belt with her mangled fingers, not caring when she ripped two nails straight from their beds. Air finally came in shallow, short bursts when she slipped her bloody fingers under the strap and pulled it away from her throat just enough to prevent it from cutting off her oxygen. Claire held firm until her fingers brushed against the bones in her exposed jaw. Her jagged teeth made her jump, but touching her tongue through the hole in her cheek repulsed her. Without thinking, she jerked her hands from the belt. The Licker tightened the strap. Her vision blurred. Dim yellow lamps above them dotted the sky like jaundiced fireflies until they entered the food court. Claire whimpered as bright white florescent lights stung her eyes.

"I can't see," she cried.

"Too bad." He dumped her on the ground like a sack of potatoes and walked past the tables. He lifted a plastic cafe chair and threw it in her direction, not close enough to hit her but close enough to make her think it might.

Claire cried.

"What are you doing?" she begged.

He ignored her. He hurled two more chairs over Claire's head. Again she begged for his plan. He flipped a table.

"What monster wants to hurt little girls?" Claire asked, her words mushy. Blood sprayed across the concrete as she spoke.

The Licker froze with another chair over his head. He brought it over to Claire and slammed it down in front of her. He sat, paused for a beat, then slid from the chair to the ground next to her, smushing his rubber tongue against her forehead.

"You aren't little girls," he said.

"What?"

"You called yourself a little girl. You aren't. You're practically grown."

"We're seventeen! Lolly is still sixteen!"

"You mean, was sixteen."

Claire moaned. The Licker pushed himself onto his elbows and stroked her hair.

"One more year to be kids, then you're off to school, right? Y'all will be adults in college. What were you going to be when you grew up, Claire? An Olympian?"

"I don't know," Claire sobbed. "I don't know."

"Probably won't be able to hold your breath underwater anymore. You'd need a cheek for that. Don't worry. It won't matter."

He pulled Claire onto the chair and used the belt to secure her upright. As he dragged her, chair and all, to the row of food carts, he rambled.

"Not everyone has choices, Claire. Not everyone has a bright future on the horizon ahead. The clock is running out for some people. It's running out for me. Maybe it ran out a long time ago."

"What do you mean?"

The Licker punched her torn cheek. Red and purple fireworks exploded in her vision. "Don't interrupt me," he snarled.

"I'm sorry," she sobbed. "I'm so sorry."

He patted her on the head. "There's no happy ending for me. I threw it all away."

"Why is that my fault?"

The Licker stopped next to a pink and blue cotton candy machine. He shoved his face in hers. Dark, shiny orbs darted back and forth beneath the webbing over his eyes, revealing a bit of the human behind the mask.

"It's not your fault," he said. "I'm pissed off, and what you're witnessing is me doing my best to feel better."

He walked around the cart, rubbing his fingers around the rim of the large silver bowl. He knelt and dug through the shelves below. "Here we go," he said, holding up a white carton. A cartoon clown on the box smiled at Claire. The design looked dated, like something from the 1950s.

A red switch blinked on the side of the machine. The Licker smacked it with his palm, and its motor hummed like the engine on Claire's grandmother's classic Mustang. He shook the carton at Claire and made a big show of pouring the fine, pastel pink powder into the bowl. He raised the box high to extend the sugar stream, cranked a knob on the front of the machine all the way to the right, and a meter twitched as it preheated.

"It has to get hot enough to melt the sugar," he said. "Are you big on baking? Nah, probably not. You look like you've never eaten so much as a mini cupcake. You'd have to live off chicken breast and spinach for a body like yours, right? So much muscle for a girl."

The cotton candy machine growled. The meter twitched back and forth, slowly edging to the right. Claire realized she was reading a thermometer.

It bobbed between 200 and 225 degrees, inching toward 300. Toasted vanilla wafted in the air.

The Licker waved his hand over the bowl like a witch with a cauldron. "Boiling water is hot. Melted sugar is molten," he said. "A sugar burn is excruciating, and it's syrupy, so it sticks to the skin. Uh oh. Here we go."

He dipped a gloved hand into the bowl and pulled out a light strand.

"Want some fresh cotton candy?" he asked.

"No!" screamed Claire. She struggled against the belt as she tried to rock the chair.

"Open your mouth," he said.

When she refused, he took his index and middle fingers and jammed them into the gash in her cheek. The flavors of blood and sweet flossy sugar mixed and made her gag.

"Please," she said. Only the consonants made it through the mush.

He replied with a fist to her face. Her nose broke with an audible crack.

Claire was too stunned to move. When he lifted her from the chair, her head spun too fast to fight. He pressed on her back and wrapped his fingers around her throat. He lowered her toward the motor in the center of the bowl. It squealed as it spun as fast as her head, maybe faster.

The heat hit her skin before the sugar. Melted candy strands licked her face, leaving red zebra stripes. He'd been right; it stuck to her skin, layering upon itself, growing fluffier and thicker as he rubbed her face clockwise around the bowl.

She resisted, albeit weakly, from the moment he pressed her face into the bowl to the moment she passed out from the pain. No one would take Claire Smithson out without a fight.

Her vision went first; the cocoon he'd spun around her head was the last thing she saw. Her hearing went next; the machine's echo stopped whirring in her ears. Sugar burned against her skin until her pain receptors short-circuited, and she went numb.

Her nose went last. When everything went silent, black, and cold, the scent of sticky, sweet, burnt sugar still lingered in her final thoughts.

When Claire lay limp long enough, The Licker raised his mask, peeled a wad of cotton candy off the corpse's head, and ate it.

CHAPTER 20

"Violet, did you hear the sound that time?" Gracie asked. We were still fumbling around inside the midway, listening as someone howled in pain.

"Yeah," I said. "You're right. That's Claire."

Gracie and I stood in the mini bowling booth, huddled together, shaking.

"Are we going to die?" she asked.

"No," I lied.

"Yes, we are. If this guy can overpower Claire, who is solid muscle and is training to drag a fucking Hummer, you and I don't have a shot in hell."

"It's not about physical strength," I lied again. "We're smarter than him."

"Lolly was smarter than both of us put together."

I hesitated. "The Licker surprised her."

"Bullshit."

It *was* bullshit. Every positive word I'd spoken since we entered the carnival was bullshit. I didn't even believe myself when I said we'd be okay, how could I convince someone else?

"I'm scared," I said.

"I want my mom," said Gracie.

I wanted my mom too. She would've been at home, asleep. Usually, she expected me to text her hourly if I was out past ten, but she'd made a special exception for the Scavenge. She didn't want to ruin my fun. She asked me to send her pictures from breakfast and bring home two sides of crispy bacon and a lemon crepe when I returned home. My lower lip trembled.

"Are we done?" I asked. "Should we hide the best we can and wait?"

"He'll find us. He's had no trouble so far. It's like he can teleport."

"Maybe it's two people."

"Multiple killers?" she cried, her voice cracking. "Jesus Christ, I couldn't wrap my head around one person wanting us dead. What could we have done to two?"

"Nothing. No one deserves this."

A crash silenced her for a moment. Two more crashes followed, further in the distance.

"He moves fast," said Gracie. "It sounded a mile away."

"No," I said. "The first crash echoed. He hasn't gotten far."

We leaned forward a bit as we waited for more screams. When it seemed like they had stopped, we relaxed, until Claire's wails filled the night as she begged for mercy.

"He's killing her," Gracie said, eyes wide.

I pressed my hand against my lips.

"I know," I said. "And we're next."

We decided that Claire was most likely near the food court at the back of the carnival. If we escaped the midway within the next five or ten minutes, we'd be able to get to the guard stand before The Licker could find us. As long as Claire continued to scream, we were safe.

Gracie gripped my hand so tightly my fingers went numb. I led her like a little child.

We took three rights around an apple bobbing booth.

"This is a full circle," I said. "It's pointless."

"There's a cajun spice flavored Pop-A-Corn stand if we go forward from here," Gracie said, pointing.

"Didn't we pass a cajun stand before?"

"Peanut butter flavor."

"Are you sure?"

"Nope."

I pulled her toward the popcorn cart anyway because I had no other idea what to do.

We had two options at the cart: run along another short row, or look behind curtain number one because the wall next to us was nothing but black plastic shower curtains hanging from a wire.

"Crawling through curtains worked in the House of Horrors," Gracie said. "Could work here too."

"I have the layout of the House memorized. Anything could be behind that plastic. We could end up twice as turned around."

"I'm willing to take a chance," said Gracie. She pulled the curtains apart, took my hand, and we stepped through into an empty booth.

A red and white dartboard surrounded by yellow flashbulbs blinked across the way. Gracie smiled.

"Come on," she said. "River is in love with the guy who owns the dart game. I've been here a thousand times. There's a pretzel cart to the left, then we turn right, then right again, then we'll exit by the dunk tank. We'll head for the guard stand and go out the employee entrance door where we came in."

Back at the food court, Claire's sounds were thicker, wetter, fewer, and far between.

Gracie led the way, breaking into a run and whipping around the corner, almost taking out the kissing booth.

We stepped out into the open. Ahead, bright lights lit up the giant apple at the entrance to the carnival. We saw it, unlinked, and ran side by side to the door.

As we approached, I could make out something on the gate. A navy sack, like a laundry bag, was tied to the bars over the employee entrance. When we got closer, I saw a leather belt wrapped tight around the middle. My eyes drifted down, I realized the bag had feet, and my own feet stopped moving.

Gracie paused to check me. "Violet, we gotta keep going." She pinched my tricep and attempted to drag me away. I stood firm.

"We can't go out the door," I said.

"Why not?"

"How much can you see without your glasses?"

"Basically nothing unless it's right in my face."

"Okay," I said. "I have perfect vision, and Ted, minus his head, is hanging on the gate."

Gracie whipped her head toward Ted. *"What?"* she asked.

Chicken skin speckled the back of my neck. I shivered despite the humidity. We had an audience, and our audience knew we'd try to escape.

I forced myself to move. Gracie followed.

"I can't touch a dead body," I whispered.

"What if your life depends on it?"

"Can you move him?"

"No."

"Why not?"

"Because I can't touch a dead body either," Gracie said. "Is there a way to go around him?"

"Might as well check."

When we got close enough, Gracie's vision came to focus, and she gasped. "Why is his neck stump so shiny?"

I ignored her. "His hands are behind his back," I said. I leaned in as close as I could manage without gagging and examined him. "The Licker tied him around the bars. We will have to cut him free if we want to get through."

"Maybe we should try it. There could be scissors or a utility knife or something in the guard stand."

"We'd need bolt cutters," I said. "He's bound with chains, not rope."

"Shit. Fine. We can't be out in the open like this. Let's get in the stand and lock ourselves in."

Gracie turned away, but I didn't. Ted's name badge had come unpinned and threatened to fall into his breast pocket. A roll of orange fabric tucked into the pocket popped out enough to hold the badge into place.

"There's something in his pocket," I said. I reached for the fabric. Ted's name badge fell into my hand. I put it in my pocket, took the orange roll from his, and stretched the material taut.

Gracie stood at the guard stand door, trying to get in.

"What is it?" she asked.

"This," I said, handing it to her.

"Screwed Tour 2017," she read. "Ted is a punk fan?"

"No. James is. We go to Screwed every summer. This is a patch from her jacket from the first year we went."

Gracie crumpled the patch in her hand and pressed it to her heart. "Are you okay?" she asked.

"No," I said.

"Goddamn it," she said. She shook the doorknob. "This thing is locked. Why wouldn't it be?"

Gracie slammed her body into the door several times.

"Let's hit it together," I said.

We took a step back and counted to three. On three, we struck it at full force.

It didn't budge.

"Can you pick a lock?" I asked.

"No. I have a bobby pin, though. Maybe it's like the movies? A little wiggle?" Gracie reached behind her ear and produced the promised pin.

I asked if she had a credit card.

"Yes!" she gasped and tossed the bobby pin on the ground. "A card is probably easier."

She pulled a slim wallet out of her crossbody bag. Hello Kitty peeked at me from an apple embossed on the red patent leather. Gracie dug through her wallet and produced a library card. She handed it to me.

"You want me to try?" I asked.

"Mmmhmm." Gracie nodded.

I knelt on the ground and peered into the crack between the door and the frame. The pieces of the lock were visible, but I didn't understand the mechanics.

"I'm supposed to use the card to press against the curved part, right? Like, push it in?"

"Do whatever your little heart tells you," she said. "Please hurry."

I slid the card in and wriggled it back and forth.

"Claire isn't making sounds anymore," I said without looking up.

"Yeah."

"Do you think Blythe is okay?" I asked.

Gracie didn't answer.

"I don't think she's okay either," I said. My chest felt hollow. "Or James. She'd die before she'd let anyone rip her jacket apart."

"What if we're the only ones left?" Gracie asked.

"We'll be testifying at this asshole's trial."

The library card slipped into place. I lifted it, and the door opened.

"You got it?" Gracie asked.

"I got it! I got it!" I said a little too loudly.

We slipped inside the office and locked the door behind us.

Gracie watched the window while I scrambled for the phone. I lifted the receiver.

Silence.

"He cut the phone," I said.

Gracie glanced over her shoulder. "Of course he did," she said flatly. "Why wouldn't he?"

I dug through the creaky metal desk drawers. Poor old Ted must've had a cell phone somewhere, but it wasn't in the guard stand.

I shook the mouse to wake Ted's computer.

"No internet connection," I told Gracie.

She stared out the window, silent, shaking.

A loud click was followed by silence, and everything went dark.

"Why does he have to keep fucking with the lights?" Gracie asked.

"To scare us," I said. "It's working. Step away from the window."

I sat on the floor under the desk and held out a hand for Gracie. She took it and crawled in with me. We sat in the blue shadows, listening to each other breathe.

Outside, something hit the side of the guard stand. A flat smack hit the exterior wall, followed by a scraping drag on the brick. Footsteps pounded on the ground as the culprit ran away.

Gracie's eyes tripled in size. Her breathing quickened. I shook my head to tell her no, it was not time to panic. I wriggled further under the desk, folded myself in half, and told Gracie to do the same.

Her face was inches from mine. I could smell her salty sweat, could feel the grit on her skin between my fingers without even touching her. We stared into each other's eyes until she broke eye contact.

"Stop it," she said.

"What?" I asked.

"Trying to read my mind."

Of all the girls there that night, Gracie and I knew each other the least. We were more than acquaintances, but not quite friends. As far as I could recall, we'd only been alone together once before.

"You know Casa de Flores?" I asked her.

"The flower shop on Belldam Boulevard?"

"Yeah. Do you remember what you told me about it?"

Gracie scowled. She used the hem of her shirt to dab her skin, smacked her lips, and sniffed.

"I remember," she said. "Why mention it now?"

River and I became friends while working on school plays together. I played first chair violin in the pit, and she built sets. Except for the year peer pressure forced her to be in *Hairspray*, Gracie didn't participate in theater. She came to all our rehearsals anyway to wait for River. She'd sit third-row center and tap away at her laptop, oblivious to the world. I figured she probably hated us all, and the computer was her invisibility cloak. River insisted that Gracie was just shy and busy with homework.

One night my mom got stuck at work and asked me to find another way home. James was long gone, so I asked River.

"Gracie drove today," she said. "She can drop you off, it's not like you live far away."

"Gracie and I aren't close enough to ask for favors."

"Oh boo. She doesn't bite."

"Will you please ask her?"

"You're such a chicken."

"Please?"

River rolled her eyes and asked Gracie if she'd take me home, Gracie agreed, though she seemed confused about why I hadn't asked for myself.

After rehearsal, on the way to the student lot, River's phone rang. Her mom had found her stash, and she'd blown up.

"She acts all high and mighty," River said when we got in the car. "She and my dad are huge stoners too. One time my dad gave me a tenth of a brownie! We bonded over it!"

"Did they throw all your weed away?" asked Gracie.

"No. I've got six or seven hiding spots. She only found one. I still need you to drop me off first. They'll kill me if I'm not home soon."

Gracie got us there in record time. When River's house came into view, Gracie pressed the brake and slowed down so River could jump out. River tumbled onto her lawn and waved to show she was okay.

"Get up here and shut the door," Gracie told me. I climbed into the front seat and slammed the passenger side door shut.

"You don't stop your car?" I asked, shocked.

"No. It started as a joke. I threatened to toss her out onto the highway because she wouldn't stop playing old Madonna songs. She said she was tough enough to survive, even though I was going sixty. Later we drove past her house, and she flung herself out of the car and didn't get a scratch on her. Now she does it all the time."

"Aren't you scared she'll hurt herself?

"It's River. She's rubber."

Gracie turned the radio on at such a low level I couldn't make out the song. The unintelligible buzz set my teeth on edge. I don't usually mess with stuff in people's cars, but the noise irritated me, and I needed to keep my hands busy. I pulled open a little cubby by the reading light. A small, stuffed bunny popped out. It had a pink ribbon necklace and comically oversized buck teeth.

"She's my little sister's," Gracie said. "A Happy Meal toy. Her name is Mint."

I lifted the bunny to my nose and sniffed. It smelled musty, not minty.

Gracie side-eyed me, so I put the bunny back and closed the cubby.

We sat in silence at a red light. I stared out my window at the shops.

Casa de Flores always had an advertisement for free flowers on their sign. That day it read:

IF YOUR NAME IS BETHANNY COME IN FOR A FREE ROSE!

"Have they ever had your name?" I asked.

"Nope," she said. "I'm glad too."

"Why?"

"I noticed something weird. You can't call me crazy if I tell you. Promise you won't."

I raised my right hand. "Swear."

Gracie told me she passed the shop every afternoon on her way home from school. The name on the sign usually changed once or twice a month.

One day the previous February, the sign promised a free rose to anyone with the name Zarrah. She said the name to herself a few times, over pronouncing the Z and rolling the Rs.

The following week, Gracie found a flier taped to a pillar outside HEB. A photo of a girl with a sunny smile was printed above several lines of text:

MISSING SINCE FEBRUARY 27TH
ZARRAH KRAMER
26 YEARS OLD
BROWN HAIR/EYES
5'3
120 POUNDS
LAST SEEN LEAVING HOME FOR WORK

Gracie felt deja vu. She said Zarrah's name out loud, over pronouncing the Z and rolling the Rs.

She shrugged it off and forgot about it until May when the sign changed:

IF YOUR NAME IS LAURYN COME IN FOR A FREE ROSE!

The barista at Grave Dirt Coffee, where Gracie and River spent their free time, was named Lauryn. Gracie didn't really like coffee, so Lauryn would mix syrups and sauces to find something she wouldn't find gagworthy.

Lauryn's name had been on the Casa de Flores sign for weeks when Gracie mentioned it to her. Lauryn laughed and said she'd seen the sign too, and she joked the message was for at her.

"They found out I'm addicted to dahlias, and they're trying to lure me in to get all my money," she said.

Gracie encouraged her to get her rose.

She never saw Lauryn again. Some neighbors found her body at the foot of her entry stairs at her apartment. Another barista told River that Lauryn's heel broke, and she tumbled down the concrete stairs right onto her neck.

Gracie still didn't put two and two together, until one day when the sign read "Alex." She knew at least a dozen people named Alex, both male and female.

Including her mother's executive assistant.

Gracie came home one day to find her mother sobbing at their kitchen island. Alex had died in a car wreck the night before.

"My mind immediately went to Zarrah and Lauryn. All three were on the sign, all three died."

I'd read about Zarrah Kramer. "The police said she ran off with her boyfriend," I told Gracie. "Lauryn's story is sad, but Alex could totally be a coincidence because, like you said, there are tons of people named Alex."

She picked at the steering wheel.

"River doesn't believe me either."

I winced. "It's not that I don't believe you. I don't want you to be freaked out about something when it probably means nothing. People whose names were on the sign are dying, that's true, but maybe you're putting together a pattern that isn't really there."

When Gracie dropped me off, I felt like a dick. After that, whenever we hung out, I'd have random flashes of our conversation, wishing it had gone differently.

"Your story was hard to believe," I told Gracie. "Flower shop murders. Kinda crazy."

"Why are you telling me this right now?"

"You're not crazy. I'm sorry if I made you feel that way."

"Why are you telling me this right now?" she repeated, her voice shaky.

"James' family does this thing. They always say stuff like 'If I die while I'm gone, I love you' when one of them leaves. No one actually expects it to be the last time they'll see each other, it's a 'in case' thing. I need you to know, in case something happens, I never thought you were crazy. A killer flower shop is too much for me. It's easier to ignore it, and it was bitchy for me to wave your feelings away."

"So you're atoning?" Gracie asked. "Because you called me nuts, and now we're going to die?"

"I guess. I'm sorry."

"It's fine. You didn't cause any real harm. River, on the other hand, called the shop and tried to get them to put my name on the sign. She makes fun of me a lot, but the whole thing gave her ammo to be a total asshole for months. It lasted until Ever got suspended for blowing Mark Booth in the band room. River moved on to teasing Ever, and I never mentioned Casa de Flores again. I decided I'd lost my mind. I even changed my route home. I never drive by there anymore."

"Scared your name will be there?" I asked.

"Kinda."

"James and I drove past yesterday. They're offering free roses to Scott right now."

"Poor Scott."

"Right?" I said. "I'm sorry River acted like an ass. She gave you shit because she loved you."

"Can we please not refer to anyone in the past tense? I can't…"

I hugged her.

"Okay," I said.

Gracie hugged me back. We sat there, holding on for dear life, trying not to cry. When she had herself under control, she pulled away, shifted into a squat, and surveyed the room.

"Are those books on the floor from a struggle, maybe?" Gracie asked.

A pile of puzzle books and a daily calendar had been tossed in a heap across the room. The threadbare carpet next to the mess of books was spattered with brown dots.

"Yeah," I said. "And the brown stuff is dried blood."

Gracie scooted sideways, away from the pile.

"What about that?" she asked, pointing.

A small radio connected to a microphone sat next to the computer tower.

A CB radio.

I got up to examine it. I'd never used one before. I didn't even know if I could turn it to a channel people could hear outside the carnival. Still, we should take a shot, so I flipped buttons until a red light came on and it buzzed.

A round dial with notches labeled 1-10 was next to the red light.

I clicked it to the first notch and pushed the button on the microphone.

"Hello?" I said, picturing my words floating into the ether.

"Hello? We're at the Poison Apple Halloween Carnival. There's a killer. Please call the police. We need help."

I turned the dial to two and repeated myself. Gracie stood and paced the small room as I pled for help on all ten channels over and over.

"You're shouting into the void," she said.

"Someone might hear us. We don't know for sure."

"We do know The Licker is out there, and he's coming for us."

I scanned the room, praying that a phone had somehow materialized in the five minutes since my last search. I pulled the desk drawers out and dumped their contents on the ground. Gracie kicked through the dried out highlighters, old wadded up pages from a daily calendar, and loose almonds.

"What are you looking for?" she asked.

"Cell phone."

"You're probably not going to find one."

"No," I said. I opened another drawer. "Here are fifty goddamn cell phone chargers, though."

"We're going to have to run," she said.

I slammed the drawer shut. *"Why?"* I shrieked. *"Why would we do that?"*

"Violet. *Chill.*"

"No," I said. I cracked an almond under my heel and ground it into the carpet. "We're waiting here until morning when Ted's replacement comes. We're safe in here."

"Really?" Gracie asked. She knocked on the window. "Doesn't sound like shatterproof glass to me. It sounds like normal glass, and it sounds pretty thin. He's going to bust in with a chainsaw or something any second."

We looked out the window, barely able to see anything. In the distance, the lights in the back of the carnival flicked on. Then a chunk of lights next to those, closer to us lit up. Section after section turned on like a wave rolling in until it crashed into the guard stand.

We stood in a spotlight with The Licker somewhere out there watching us, waiting for us to perform.

"Gracie, please," I begged.

"I'm sorry, Violet. I can't die in a room that smells like feet and old coffee. Maybe there's a spot out back by the Whirling Witch where we can slip through the gate. I swear the bars are wider apart over there."

"No," I begged. "No, no, no. Don't leave me."

"Yes, yes, yes. Please come. We're safer together, we're safer on the move."

Gracie didn't wait for me to reply. She put her hand on the knob, gave me a nod, and opened the door. The fear of being alone outweighed the fear of being out in the open, so without thinking, I ran past her, and immediately stepped into a hole. My ankle twisted, and I slammed into the ground.

"Shit," I said through gritted teeth.

"Check yourself," she whispered. "Check yourself and make sure you're okay."

Gracie pulled me to my feet. I wiggled my extremities, anticipating pain. My ankle stung, but my head, neck, arms, and legs were fine.

In my peripheral vision, The Licker stomped toward us.

"Gracie," I said, choking back tears. "He's behind us. Gracie."

"Keep moving," she told me. "Don't turn around."

But she ignored her own advice, and she did exactly that.

Gracie glanced over her shoulder. The sight of him shook her. She stumbled, missed a step, and fell at my feet. She landed on the ankle I'd twisted. I howled.

The Licker laughed as I lost my balance and landed on Gracie. We were a tangle of limbs and hair, tearing each other back down each time we scrambled to stand. She finally made it to her feet, steadied herself, and tried to lift me one last time. I was halfway up when an axe flew past my right ear and hit her squarely in the chest.

Blood exploded from her mouth and dripped onto my face.

I hugged her again, this time to slow her fall.

"I want my mom," she whispered. "I want my Mommy."

The light in Gracie's eyes went out, the quick flip of a switch. No struggle, no drawn out suffering.

I didn't want to leave her there. I had no choice.

"Don't run Violet," The Licker said. "I promise I won't hurt you."

CHAPTER 21

When a murderer in a rubber mask tells you *not* to run, *you should move like your ass is on fire.*

Fortunately, that's what I did.

I headed straight for the carousel, intending to hide until I could swing back to the entrance and get the hell out of the carnival. I wanted to be worried about my friends, especially James, since she'd been MIA since we first split up.

But the time had come and gone for saving everyone else.

Air whipped my face as I ran, giving me a chill. The August heat mixed with sweat caused by visceral panic left me soaked. My shirt clung to my skin, a fine mist of sweat covered my face. A shiver nauseated me. I couldn't breathe.

"You can't outrun me, Violet," The Licker said. "You're too out of shape, my skinny fat queen!"

I grunted in response. If I'd had the energy to be offended by his remark, I would've been pissed.

Robotic static rang through the carnival as The Licker laughed.

I guesstimated that he was about three car lengths behind me. If I were going to lose him, I would need to go somewhere packed with hiding places. Ideally, the midway would've been an option, but I wasn't going to risk getting lost again.

The arcade was the next best choice.

A Choo Choo Train whistle cheerfully signaled the Black Kitten Coaster to run as I sprinted past the ride. A chain of rotten zombie worms gently rolled over tiny hills at a moderate pace, their grimacing faces faded from the sun. It was the only roller coaster I'd ever ridden, and I'd only ridden it once. At the end, there was a small rise and fall, honestly less scary than riding in a car with Blythe behind the wheel, but it still almost made me pee my pants.

"If you're going to hide in the arcade, don't bother," The Licker yelled.

Playing the "opposite game" with him had worked in my favor so far. Fire filled my lungs as my feet pounded the grass, propelling me faster than I'd ever moved in my life, straight into the arcade.

A hurricane had blown through the room. Broken glass glittered on the ground. Games were knocked on their sides. Teddy bears were ripped in half; their skins rested on piles of cloud-like stuffing.

I fell to the ground and crawled behind the ticket counter. My fingers twitched; I had to lock my hands as if in prayer to stop them.

"I already played hide and seek in here with River," he said. "I'm bored with that game."

My skin crawled at the realization River's body might be close. I couldn't take seeing another corpse.

The Licker kicked the mess on the floor as he stalked the arcade. Every few steps, he would stop. When he stopped, I held my breath. A broken game had vomited a pile of wires and circuitry onto the tile. I listened as he shuffled through it. He stopped at the counter.

I felt him lean over to peek at me in my hiding spot.

"Look up," he said.

My eyes drifted to the ceiling.

To the *mirrored* ceiling.

The Licker's reflection gave me a little wave.

"Shit," I shouted. It didn't matter if he heard me.

"Shit is right," he said. "I told you not to come in here. Word to the wise, when you start running again, avoid the mirror maze. Too dark. Don't try to hide in the souvenir shops either. Or in the House of Horrors. In fact, don't hide at all. I'm not going to hurt you."

"Why?" I asked.

"You remind me of me."

My brain broke while wondering what part of my personality screamed spree killer.

I pulled myself together enough to take my shot.

"If you're not going to hurt me, can I leave?" I asked.

The Licker didn't respond right away. He rapped his knuckles on the glass, causing the whole counter to shake. He breathed into his voice changer, a perfect imitation of Darth Vader.

"No," he finally said. "You can't. You'll tell."

"I don't even know who you are. You're wearing a mask."

"You'll tell people what happened. You saw everything."

"If you're not going to kill me, and you're not going to let me go, what then?"

"You can come with me when I'm done."

I considered the words. If he hadn't finished, someone was still alive.

"You want me to go to a second location with you and your nasty ten-inch tongue?"

"Some girls are into that."

"Gross."

Silence.

I shifted my body.

The Licker stood straight.

I squatted and prepared to run.

A near toxic cocktail of adrenaline, fear, and stupidity helped me leapfrog over the counter. I laughed when I landed safely. He tilted his head, surprised by my move.

I ran from the arcade past the worms, which had frozen on the hump that terrified me so much. I wished for the days when a drop on a coaster made for toddlers was still my biggest fear.

Until then, I hadn't even thought of hiding in the souvenir shops. Now I was headed straight for the photo store, the little hut where happy carnival goers could purchase pictures snapped during their visit.

As soon as the door closed behind me, it hit me.

He'd told me exactly where he wanted me to go.

"I'm so stupid, I deserve to die," I whispered.

I pressed against the wall, ready for him to walk through the door.

But he didn't.

I waited.

He still didn't appear and didn't make a sound outside.

It was time for the big jump scare. I'd relax, and he'd burst through wielding a chainsaw.

Minutes passed.

The door remained shut.

I scanned the room for another way out. There was no other exit or even a back office where I could hide.

I slid along the wall toward the print station. A collection of photos dangled from the ceiling like Christmas ornaments. I'd seen them a thousand times before, happy couples on the Ferris Wheel, little kids hollering as they ran from the House of Horrors, a baby grimacing while eating a sour pickle as big as his head.

Or that's what the pictures should've been.

Instead, I saw my own face.

I sat at the edge of a chair, violin under my chin, eyes sharp as my bow danced across the strings. My orchestra director's husband took it at a rehearsal for the spring musical. It was the only picture of myself I'd ever put online.

Next to me, a photo of River and Gracie floated back and forth. Bright smiles lit their faces as they held the contract they'd signed with their publisher.

We were all there.

Claire kissing a gold medal.

James posing with her laptop on her head, eyes crossed.

Blythe squinting in a sunny selfie, her hot pink bikini glowing even hotter against her tan skin.

Mila flying through the air in a split.

Lolly giving a speech about climate change to elementary school students.

"He set us up on purpose," I whispered.

I knew he'd targeted us, but I hadn't realized it was so personal.

I plucked Mila's picture from its string and examined it. A stamp on the back told me it was printed at the carnival in late June. The Licker had planned this night for months.

I jumped when someone knocked on the door. The photo fell from my hand and landed on the ground. Mila smiled at me, arms over her head in triumph.

The person on the other side of the door knocked again, then scratched at the door like a dog.

"What kind of killer knocks before entering?" I wondered.

The scratching stopped. The person on the other side slapped the door and screamed my name.

Knowing full well I could be walking into a trap, I opened the door.

Long arms reached for me. I stepped back.

Blythe fell to the ground, laughing.

"Why didn't you save me?" she asked. "I would've saved you."

CHAPTER 22

"Violet?" Blythe whined. "You let me fall. Why am I down here?"

I could tell she thought she was whispering.

"God," I said. "You're in worse shape than before."

"This is all a dream," she said. "It's so weird."

"It's not a dream."

I tried in vain to get her on her feet. When I pulled her arms, she jerked them away and rolled into a ball.

"No, it's a dream," she insisted. "I fell asleep in that box. Where is everyone?"

I didn't want to freak her out, so I told her they were hiding.

"Someone is trying to hurt us. You have to be quiet."

I placed a finger on her lips to shush her. She yelped in pain.

"Nooooooooo. I can't. I'm sooooo dizzy, and my leg hurts. Oh! We can run away! Carry me piggyback!"

Blythe was 5'10. I was 5'4. Imagining her on my back with her toes dragging the ground made me chuckle.

"I can't carry you. You'll have to stay here."

I searched the room for something to barricade the door. The best thing I could find was a tall metal stool. I tried to jam it under the doorknob. It was about an inch too short.

"Remember the night we drove and saw the bats?" Blythe asked.

"The bats?" I asked.

"Austin bats."

"Oh. Yeah."

A bat colony roosted under a bridge in Austin. Every evening, over a million little monsters would wake up and fly into the sky to spend their night snacking on bugs while dangerously blocking the views of people driving in the area.

One night after Blythe got her Tesla, she, Lolly, and I drove into the city to watch them take flight.

We stood on the bridge, Lolly in the middle, and watched batty black dots fly against the orange sherbet sky.

"This is the largest colony in the world," Lolly told us. "Most are female."

"Can you enjoy a moment without researching it?" asked Blythe.

Lolly tilted her head. "Learning is half the fun."

Blythe rolled her eyes. She got her phone out and snapped a few dozen photos. At one point, she turned the phone over to me to get some shots of her against the setting sun. I'd become quite the photographer thanks to Blythe.

"Can you come over next to me and get a profile shot?" she asked.

"You call me out for reading about stuff," said Lolly. "What about you? Can you enjoy the moment without documenting it for your followers?"

Blythe blushed and extended a hand. I passed her phone back.

"The bats are so pretty, I want to share them," she whispered in my ear.

My chest tightened. Sometimes Blythe's mask would slip, and the "real" girl behind the fame would shine through.

Now, in the photo booth, I could see her authentic self again.

Not a sweet girl wanting to share beauty, but a wasted stoner girl who couldn't comprehend the seriousness of the situation.

"I remember the bats," I told her. "Why?"

Blythe pressed her back against the door and slid to the floor. She looped an arm through the stool's legs.

"I felt like such shit that night when Lolly called me out. She wasn't wrong. It was the top, you know?"

"The top of the bridge?" I asked.

"The top of my life. People loved me back then. I made a video where I compared fifteen different clear lip glosses, and it got a million views. I posted a photo you took on the bridge, and it got so many likes and a billion comments. There were so many I couldn't reply to them all."

This was not the time for a pity party, nor was it time to reminisce about social media popularity.

"Blythe," I said calmly. "We have to leave this carnival. Someone is out there. He is going to kill us if he finds us. He already attacked you, that's why you're all beat up."

She stretched her legs out and examined the cuts and bruises.

"Oh yeah. Hey, where are the other girls?"

I knelt in front of her.

"I'm pretty sure they're all dead."

"Pretend dead?" she asked, her voice childlike.

"No," I said firmly.

"Weird."

"Very."

"Why kill us?"

I pointed to the photos. "Someone is obsessed with us."

She pushed me away and got up. She ripped a picture of herself off its string, tearing off the top in the process.

"You're all doing stuff in yours," she said frowning. "Playing your cello, Mila dancing, James being a geek. I'm in a bikini."

"It's a violin," I corrected her. She was right, though. Ours were all action shots, while hers was more cheesecake.

"Didn't you once tell me you get death threats? Do you think some creepy guy might be stalking you?"

She ignored me and traced her photo with a finger.

I repeated my question.

"Some," she sighed. "It's mostly losers with nothing better to do. We report it to the police. They never care. No one ever does anything."

I wanted to ask her if anyone threatened her more than once. I thought of The Licker at the carnival, of Heather's warning about creeps online.

"Blythe..."

A series of blood-curdling screams cut me short. Blythe whipped around, eyes wide.

"What the hell?" she asked.

My hands shook. My vision blurred. Sweat trickled down my spine.

"James," I said. I couldn't say anything else. "James," I repeated. "It's James."

Blythe mumbled to herself as She ran her hands through her somehow still perfect beachy waves. Her knuckles were purple and swollen.

"Get in the corner and don't move," I instructed.

"Why?" Blythe asked. The word came out low, her accent thicker than usual.

"Because I have to go save James."

CHAPTER 23

M y lungs burned. My legs shook. My brain pounded inside my skull.

I wasn't afraid. Not now. James was alive, I would save her, we would save Blythe, and we would be okay.

James' pleas for help echoed through the whole carnival. I could tell she was somewhere past the carousel, near the midway.

I'd never run so fast in my life. Every few steps, I glanced over my shoulder, expecting to be face to face with The Licker's horrible rubber mask. I tripped twice but didn't fall. A thousand unseen eyes fixed their gaze on me. Voices whispered in my ear.

"We should break into pairs," said Claire.

"We could get caught," Lolly said. "We could get arrested."

"These babies each have twenty milligrams of THC in them," River said.

Though it had been hours since I ate my circus peanut, the sticky melted marshmallow still coated my throat. I retched. Bile shot up my throat, flooding my nose, sending me into a coughing fit.

"Who's there?" James yelled. "Help! Please, God, help me!"

"It's me!" I yelled back.

"Violet?"

"Where are you?"

She didn't need to answer. As soon as I passed the carousel, I could see her.

She sat on a small board above the dunk tank, arms tied behind her back. Her legs dangled in the air.

Blood poured from a gash on her forehead. A shiny red and purple splotch highlighted her right cheekbone.

"Violet!" she sobbed. "Please get me down! Please! If I fall, I'll drown."

The dunk tank was a ten foot tall glass box filled with gray tinged water. The little stairs the dunkee used to climb onto the podium were gone. A big blue sign hung behind James:

LET'S GET WET AND WILD!!!

I nearly ran straight into the glass. I stopped short and hit it with my fist.

"Where are the stairs?" I asked. "Where have you been?"

"Stairs are gone. Never saw them. I woke up thirty seconds ago. My mind's blank. No memories from after we entered the carnival. Now, that's my whole life story, will you *please* get me down!"

"Dude, I can't climb glass. I need the stairs."

"Is there anything else you can use?" Her voice shook. James rarely cried. My heart stopped in fear as I watched her tears flow.

"Maybe in the midway. I'll check. Can you untie yourself?"

"Trust me bitch. I'm trying. The knots are super tight. My wrists are shredded."

I scrambled to find something I could use as a step stool. I entered the midway, far enough to eyeball at a few booths but not far enough to risk getting lost.

There was a waist-high folding table tucked behind the

counter at the basketball toss. I ripped it from the booth and dragged it back to the dunk tank.

The table swayed under me when I climbed onto the slick laminate top.

"God, don't fall," said James.

"I'm doing my best."

My best wasn't good enough. Even standing on the table, I couldn't reach the top edge.

"On a scale of one to ten, how screwed are we?" she asked.

"Thirteen," I said.

"Shit."

I got on my hands and knees and climbed off the table. Without the stairs, I couldn't save her.

"I have to get help," I said.

"You can't leave me here!"

"I don't have a choice."

James' lips quivered. All the color drained from her face.

"Please don't leave me," she begged.

I punched the tank again, this time so hard I nearly broke my fingers.

"Listen to me," I said. "I've seen this asshole in action. If he wanted you dead, you would be. But you're not. He tied you up for a reason. I'm going to go back to the Tesla and get my phone to call 911. I will be right back, and I will have cops with me."

"Violet," she said. She pressed her cheek against her shoulder to wipe away her tears. "Promise me I'm not going to drown. Promise me…"

She never finished her sentence.

She screamed, not like her cries for help before. Ear shattering, ground shaking, desperation.

Not the screams of someone who thinks she might die.

The screams of someone who *knows she will.*

I squeezed my eyes shut until I saw stars.

I took a deep breath, turned around, and opened my eyes.

The Licker had stolen James' army jacket, and he'd put it on over his cloak.

He had a screwdriver in one hand and an axe in the other.

He bolted towards us, waving the weapons above his head.

There was nowhere to run. I swallowed and prepared to meet my fate.

Then a funny thing happened.

The Licker stopped, dropped both weapons, and removed the mask. It flopped to the ground tongue first.

James stopped screaming. I gasped.

"What the," said James.

"Fuck?" I finished.

Blythe laughed as she slipped off James' jacket. She wadded it into a ball, threw it aside, and removed her cloak.

"Why are you two all worked up?" she asked, smirking. "Did I miss something?"

CHAPTER 24

An invisible fist slammed into my solar plexus, making it impossible to fill my lungs.

This wasn't real, *couldn't* be real. High-ass Blythe found the costume and put it on, obviously.

Maybe I was hallucinating.

Or maybe the whole thing was a prank. My friends joined together to scare the hell out of me as an early birthday present. I scanned the distance, hoping the other girls would pop out from behind the rides. They'd laugh, maybe film my reaction. We'd get pancakes, and they'd tell me how they hatched their plan.

But no one came.

"Violet, honey," said Blythe. She gave me a little wave and snapped her fingers. "Did I lose you for a second?"

She approached me slowly, as though I was the predator, and she didn't want me to attack.

"What's happening?" My voice cracked. I still couldn't breathe.

I backed away from her until my back pressed into the dunk tank's cool glass wall.

Above me, James repeated Blythe's name over and over again.

"Blythe?" she squealed. "Blythe? *Blythe?*"

Blythe laughed. "Blythe Blythe Blythe Blythe. You've said it so many times it's lost meaning."

"What's happening?" I repeated.

"What's happening?" Blythe asked in a mocking tone. She unclipped the chest strap on the gray backpack she'd been wearing under her cloak and dropped it on the ground. "You have no idea how hot that mask is."

Blythe unzipped the backpack and pulled out a bandana to wipe her face. She threw the bandana onto James' jacket and rummaged around in the backpack to find water. She was remarkably coordinated for someone who had downed weed edibles with a shot of liquor.

"You're not high," I said. "Or drunk."

"Nope. It's pretty easy to fake. I didn't fake these babies, though." Blythe twisted her arm to examine a massive gash on her bicep. "Those bitches totally put up a fight."

"You killed them," said James through gritted teeth. She'd stopped crying.

"Sure did. Pretty easily, too. Once the adrenaline kicks in, that's power."

"How?" I asked. Her face blurred. Maybe this wasn't really Blythe. Maybe it was a demon or some witch's magic trick. Those would make much more sense.

"Hammers and glass and dunk tanks, darling."

"Dunk tanks?" yelled James.

Blythe chuckled. "You ain't up there for the pretty view."

"You moved their bodies," I said. "You crushed Lolly's head. How could you physically do that?"

"I put on a shitload of muscle when I did a Better Booty Challenge for my YouTube channel. I can deadlift as much as Claire! You assholes didn't say a word. I walked around half-naked all the time, even to the fucking doctor's office. I wanted to see if any of you noticed my ass."

"I did," I told her. This was true. One night we hung out at

Claire's, and Blythe wore high waisted denim shorts so short her butt cheeks were on full display. I couldn't even look her in the eye that day.

"You didn't say anything," Blythe said.

"Was I supposed to?" I whispered.

"Eh," she shrugged. "No. I'm messing with you. You'd have to be crazy to kill someone because they didn't compliment your butt."

"Technically, you have to be crazy to kill someone in general."

Blythe chuckled. "Man, Violet, when did you become funny?"

"Wasn't joking."

Her face fell. "You need to get out of my way, V. James and I have unfinished business."

She reached into her backpack and dug around, her eyes never leaving mine. She expected me to fight or to run. I was too stunned to do either.

Blythe pulled a dirty softball from the bag. She tossed it in the air and caught it, then held it out to me.

"You want to do the honors?" she asked.

"*What?*"

"You have as much of a reason to be mad at these bitches as I do."

"Stop calling them bitches."

Blythe rolled her eyes. "Fine."

"What do you and I have to be mad about?" I asked.

"What did I do to you?" asked James at the same time.

"What should we be mad about? What did you do?" Blythe cackled. She made a strange gravelly noise and spun around in circles. "What did you do? You got into schools. The best schools. Scholarships, awards. Moving away, big things in bright cities."

I couldn't quite process her words.

"You're mad because they're going to college?" I asked.

"Ding, ding, ding! It's after college too." Blythe waved the softball in James' direction. "That one is probably going to found the next Google. Claire was going to win an Olympic medal. River and Gracie had a book deal for their stupid comic. Violet, I thought for sure you were off to join the New York Philharmonic or something. Guess you're not talented enough."

Those words hit as hard as Blythe's big reveal. I'd had the same thought a million times over the summer. Hearing it spoken out loud by someone else made it more real.

"You *are* talented," I said. "More than most people."

"At what?" she asked, tossing the softball from one hand to another.

"What you do. You're one of the most popular social media gurus on the planet."

"Well thanks for calling me popular, but no. I'm not. At my height, I was B-list at best, and social media influencers aren't exactly top tier celebrities, so…"

"You have so many followers," I said. "You have brand endorsements. Jesus, you had an offer for your own talk show."

"Twenty other girls got invited to meet for the talk show gig. I was their fourth choice. Guess what. Fourth place doesn't get a show. As for my endorsements, I'm not getting the good ones anymore. A company that makes cleansing oak milk sponsored my last video."

"Oat milk?" asked James.

"*Oak.* Like the tree. They squeeze it from the bark or something. I didn't care enough to ask how it's made. I drank it for a week, and my stomach hurt more than the time I ate an entire family-sized bag of hot Cheetos. I used to book high end handbags, expensive skincare. Not anymore. New people are climbing the ladder daily, people with actual talent. I have no skills. I'm not a makeup artist, I can't do interior design, and I can't bake. I make an ass outta myself for some laughs, nothing more." Blythe wiped her nose with her hand. "I hate myself," she mumbled.

"Apparently," I said. "What about all your money, though? You'd have no problem paying tuition. It's not too late to apply."

"Ha. Funny thing. I never took the SATs. I barely pass my classes. I have no extracurriculars."

"You run a business!" I screeched. "That's an extracurricular!"

"No. I buy followers. Always have. I'm a fraud. Last month some assholes 'cancelled' me and my real followers abandoned ship. My views tanked, which in turn wrecked my income. I had to stoop to calling my dad. He hired some professionals to fix everything, which turned out to be bullshit."

"Why?"

"Apparently dear old Daddy doesn't pay his taxes, and neither did I. He's been selling assets left and right. He's going to prison, and maybe I am too. Can you arrest a seventeen-year-old for tax fraud?" Her face fell, went completely blank. Her pretty features were mottled gray.

"I'm not sure," I said.

"Are we all getting the picture now?" Blythe asked. Her desperate tone rose to a squeal at the end. She was on the verge of spinning out.

To be honest, I did understand her point of view. All the other kids in school were obsessed with *starting* Senior year so they could *finish* Senior year and move on. None of them knew how much it hurt me when River and Gracie spent hours on an app hunting for their future apartment, when Claire bragged about another scout coming to a swim meet, or when Lolly had a panic attack because she was worried she wouldn't be the smartest student at her university. My heart swelled with half irritation, half soul crushing jealousy.

Never enough to murder anyone, though.

"You're right," I said. "I get it. I'm terrified about the future, and I'm such a loser compared to everyone else."

"The worst part is, no one notices," Blythe said, frowning.

"Yeah," James said. "Like they didn't notice your ass."

Blythe's left eye twitched. "Say one more fucking word, and you're dead, James!" she shrieked, waving the softball. James leaned back on the platform, lost her balance, and came dangerously close to falling.

"Please calm down," I begged.

Blythe took a breath and lowered her arm. "I don't have anyone to talk to," she said.

"You could've talked to me."

"It's embarrassing," she said, her voice shaky.

"You said we're the same," I said. "If that's true, what do you have to be embarrassed about?"

Blythe's mouth twitched at the corners, and her features softened. Then she shook her head and returned to the task at hand.

"We're different enough," she said. "You might not go to DSU, but you'll go somewhere. You'll keep playing your violin until your chin has a permanent dent, and your fingers fall off. In the end, you'll get where you want to go in life, even if you have to take the scenic route."

Her mouth twisted into a snarl. Her eye twitched again as she grew visibly more agitated with me. The future she imagined for me pissed her off, and I could feel my immunity dissipate.

"All I ever wanted was to go to DSU," I said, playing for her sympathy. "I don't have a second choice. I'll be stuck at Belldam Community College. They don't even have an orchestra."

"You'll be fine," said Blythe. "You'll be fine. James, on the other hand…"

Blythe reared back and hurled the softball at the tiny red target connected to the dunk tank. James' deafening screams made tears well in my eyes.

The softball missed the target by about two inches.

"Please don't," begged James. "I can't swim! I can't swim!"

"And water scares you shitless," Blythe said, laughing. "It's fun to watch you squirm. You should beg me."

"Beg you?" asked James.

"Yeah. For your life. It's funny."

"Let me go, and I swear to God I will grovel at your feet," James said sharply.

"No one has to know it was you," I told Blythe. "There aren't any cameras, no witnesses. There's no way anyone will believe a girl committed these murders."

Blythe pulled her phone from her back pocket. She tapped the screen and turned it around to reveal a 3x3 grid of video feeds.

"There actually are cameras. James turned them off. I turned them back on, and I've been controlling them via my phone. "

"How did you learn to do that?" asked James.

"From you," said Blythe.

James blinked. "I never gave you a lesson."

"You're always so excited to show off your mediocre hacking skills," Blythe said. "I paid attention and learned. Once I got the basics from you, I watched a few YouTube videos and read a few articles. It was easy. Is that surprising, or did you think I was too stupid to work a computer?"

"You're not stupid," James said.

Blythe smirked. "I'm sure I'm a fucking genius from where you sit now, huh?"

She slid her phone back in her pocket and walked toward the tank. She held out a finger and smiled at James. She got closer and closer to the red target. James shook her head, her lip trembling. Blythe brushed the target with a finger. We all held our breath to see if James' seat would drop. When it didn't, Blythe waved her hand in front of the target, laughing.

"We'll lie for you!" I promised. "We'll burn the mask and say we chased the killer off."

Blythe stopped waving and crossed her arms over her chest.

"Interesting proposition," she said.

"Please," said James. "We'll say we never saw the killer without his mask."

"You two would seriously do that? Let me ride off into the sunrise after I killed six people?"

"Yes," I said. I meant it, too. I'd have done anything to walk out of there alive, done anything to keep James safe. "We can't bring them back."

"You're not a teeny bit concerned I might try to finish the job later? Like maybe I'll sneak into your house and hide in your closet with a knife? Poison could be fun too. I researched 'how to poison someone' at the library in Austin for hours awhile back. At the time, I decided it wasn't for me. I wanted to play a more active role, not sit back and let rat poison do it for me."

"What if you agree to see someone?" I asked. "If you go to a therapist and maybe get on some meds, it'll be fine."

Blythe walked toward me. Each foot hit the ground with an earth-shaking thud. She took my hand and intertwined our fingers. My intestines nearly slid out of my body.

"I love you, Violet. You'd do anything for a friend, wouldn't you." She nodded in James' direction.

"Friends," I said. "Plural. I'll do anything for you, too."

She squeezed my hand, three quick pulses, each one progressively harder. She twisted my wrist until it popped and pinned my arm against my back. I doubled over in pain.

"We were never that close," she said, her jaw locked. "You'd sell me out in a second. You'd probably do it the second the cops got here. I'm not an idiot. And I'm not done yet."

She let me go and pushed me to the ground.

Above me, James hyperventilated. I wanted to hug her.

"Please don't hurt me," she pleaded.

Blythe paced. She rolled her head from side to side and flapped her hands.

My eyes drifted to the screwdriver Blythe had tossed aside. One stab through an eye, through a temple, or straight through the heart would take her out.

"What are you doing?" Blythe asked me.

"Nothing."

"Go for it," she said. "I dare you."

"No."

She snatched the screwdriver and threw it into the dark carnival.

"You're such a little fighter, trying to find a weapon. I respect that. Maybe we *could* strike a deal."

A heavy weight lifted off my shoulders. Light glowed at the end of the tunnel.

"Yes," I said. "Anything. *Anything.*"

"I'm going to ask you a question. Something you should be able to answer if you've ever paid attention to what I say. If you get it right, I won't drown James."

"Okay!" I exclaimed. "I listen to you. I really do."

Blythe pulled a second softball out of her backpack.

"If you get it wrong..."

She waved the ball in the air, her arm a snake slithering toward me.

"I won't," I promised.

"Hmm," she said. "What do I even ask? This wasn't part of my plan."

"Something about your videos?" I suggested.

Blythe smiled. "You watch them?"

"Yes," I lied. Her videos had gotten far too repetitive, and I didn't bother wasting my time. "All your videos."

"I never knew," she said. "The other girls don't watch my stuff."

"I do," said James.

"I don't believe you for one second," Blythe snapped. "And, once again, shut the fuck up. This game is for Violet, not you." She frowned, her brow furrowed. She stopped pacing. She stared at the Whirling Witch Coaster. At some point, she'd turned the lights off. She pulled her phone back out. "You would not believe how easy it was to figure out the lights. A college student does maintenance on the carnival's electricity. A little attention, a little cleavage, and he told me everything. I didn't even have to sleep with him."

"Would you have?" I asked.

"Probably. But I only needed a password. He gave it up faster than Mila at a football game after party."

My face burned. "Don't talk about Mila that way."

"Right, right. Shouldn't talk shit about the dead. My bad."

My stomach dropped.

Now it was confirmed, Mila was gone. Claire, Gracie, River, Lolly, all dead because Blythe lost some followers online.

Blythe tapped on her phone. Lights on the Whirling Witch Coaster blinked to life. Another tap and music played through the speakers hidden around the carnival. The weird clown song from the carousel, canned cheers from the midway, and the funeral dirge from the House of Horrors mixed into a brain splitting cacophony. I pressed my hands over my ears.

Blythe beamed, her face lit from within like a child.

"I've got it," she said. "Violet, what horrible crime did I supposedly commit that led to my cancellation?"

"What?" I had no idea what she meant.

"If you follow me online you'd know. It was a huge thing, and I had to make an hour long video groveling to twelve-year-olds. Total bullshit completely fabricated by assholes who have nothing better to do than rip other people - *people who do actual work* - apart."

I tilted my head. "You said you don't work."

Blythe took five big steps and threw herself at me.

"I never said I don't work. I work. I wrote a marketing plan, I shoot and edit my own videos, and I'm constantly promoting myself. You wouldn't believe how many asses I have to kiss. Views increase when influencers appear in each other's videos. Turns out, I hate other influencers. I have to play nice and fake it to get included. That's work. I never said I don't work. I said what I do doesn't have *value.*"

"Those are all valuable skills. Why can't you edit someone else's videos or do someone else's social media?"

"Because I don't want to. I don't want to answer to someone else. If people found out I'd stooped to editing one of these new girl's videos...there's an eighth-grader in Idaho who exclusively does daily planner supply review videos. Notebooks, stickers, and shit. I'm supposed to bend the knee for a bitch like that?"

"It would be better than *murdering your friends in cold blood.*"

Above us, James groaned. "Violet, please don't provoke the crazy bitch."

"Uh uh uh," Blythe scolded her. "I wouldn't call me names if I were you."

She turned back to me. Her eyes bulged, sweat glistened on her skin. Grease made her messy bun stringy. Runny eyeliner settled in dark circles under her eyes. Blood smears stained her cheek.

I wondered if it was her blood or someone else's.

"Tick tock, Violet. Why did I get canceled?"

I hadn't seen Blythe much that summer. While she spent the summer plotting mass murder, I spent it practicing violin and developing an ulcer over DSU. I'd barely been online. I uploaded some photos of my neighbor's Pomeranian to social media, Googled random stuff, and made music playlists.

I definitely hadn't been watching Blythe's videos.

One of the few times we hung out was on a long drive to take pictures in a bluebonnet field. The ones near Belldam weren't good enough. Blythe needed the best, and she read that the best were near Brenham.

"We can stop at the Blue Bell creamery and go on the tour," she teased. "You get free ice cream at the end."

"I mean, I can't say no to ice cream," I replied.

She invited some other girls; only James wanted to go.

We piled into the Tesla. James cracked some jokes, and I played along for a little bit until I realized Blythe seemed more quiet than usual. I asked her what was wrong. She flatly said, "Nothing."

But throughout the day, she dropped hints.

In the bluebonnets, we found a squirrel family in a little nest.

"They're so cute I could steal them and take them home," James said.

Blythe snorted. "Better leave them alone. They might not be internet approved pets."

"Internet approved pets?" I asked.

"Nevermind." she mumbled.

Later, on the way to Blue Bell, James suggested that we take a weekend trip to South Padre. She said she could get Heather to chaperone.

"Ugh, no," Blythe said. Her voice wavered a little, and her eyes were fixed on the road. "I can't handle any more fish."

"Did you get drunk and puke up some fish or something?" James asked, laughing.

Blythe didn't laugh back, or even smile. She scowled. At the time, I wrote it off as her being irritated with James. Her sour demeanor hung around her like a dust cloud for the rest of the day.

That night, after flowers and ice cream and weird burgers at a tiny barbecue joint in the backwoods, we dropped James off at her house. Blythe drove the car down the street, pulled over, and slammed her head into the steering wheel.

"What the hell?" I gasped.

"Everything is too much. Right? You get it?"

I had no clue what she meant, so I gave a generic response.

"Life is pretty overwhelming lately," I told her. Nothing I said would matter. She needed to vent.

"You get it. You always get it. James doesn't. She's off in La La Land with her computers. Have you ever felt like the entire world is turning against you?"

"Sure. The other day my mom was super pissed at me, James and I got into a fight, and no one else would answer my texts.

There's the whole college thing too. I'm pretty sure they hate me. Or worse, they're indifferent."

She hit her head on the steering wheel again, then grunted like a wounded animal. I looked around nervously, worried someone might be watching.

In hindsight, I should've anticipated her break with reality.

"Hey!" Present-day Blythe snapped her fingers in my face. "Where did you go?"

"Summer," I said. "The bluebonnets."

Blythe grinned. Blood rimmed her gums.

"Oh my God," she said.

"The world turned against you," I said. "Bigger than normal problems. Overwhelming."

"When you get canceled, that's generally what happens. You have no idea. I got death threats."

I had no memory of Blythe receiving death threats, but I couldn't say as much out loud. She might've addressed the threats in the apology video I didn't watch.

"I can't believe someone would threaten you for something so small," I said sympathetically.

"Right? Maybe a tweet or two to teach me, but not death threats."

"So stupid," James said.

Blythe took a breath, held it, and let it go. Her body relaxed. She dropped her head to her chest. "I'm not an idiot Violet," she said.

"What do you mean?"

"You're being vague. Why did I get canceled?"

I went blank. James' feet were dangerously close to the water. She couldn't swim, couldn't float, couldn't tread. Her hands were still bound. If she fell in, she'd drown. I placed a hand on the tank.

Then it hit me.

"You got a fish!" I yelled triumphantly. "You put it in the wrong tank, and people went crazy!"

Blythe slapped her hands together, a single crack that almost made me jump out of my skin.

"Damn fish," she said. "I won it here, over in the midway. Those assholes had a field day with it."

"You bought it a big tank," I said. I remembered the story, not because I followed her online, but because she told me in a series of voice texts after our trip to Brenham. In the first message, her voice was calm. By the ninth, she was howling, and I could hear her ripping her room to pieces in the background.

"I saved it from its claustrophobic little bowl, and I listened to the asshole at the pet store, right?" Blythe asked, panic in her voice, her hands flying in the air. She leaned in and stuck a finger in my face. "What am I supposed to do, get a Ph.D. in *fish?*"

"You'd have to get your Master's first," I said sarcastically. I immediately winced, anticipating a slap.

Blythe ignored me and continued her rant.

"People never give each other the benefit of the doubt. God, it's not like I dropped the n-word or something. It was a fucking fish. A *fish.* They die if you look at them funny. My life is worth the same as a fish's to some people. It's stunning."

I held back a snort. My freshly minted multiple murderer friend Blythe stood before me, pondering the value of human life.

"Did the fish thing make you do this?" I asked quietly.

Blythe laughed, manic and angry.

"It's the fish, it's the failure, it's all the fresh new fourteen-year-olds who grew up watching my videos and are now replacing me. It's my friends, who barely tolerate me. It's my father, who screwed me. It's my fear that I've lost at the game of life, and I haven't even graduated high school. I'm effed six ways from Sunday, and I'm so, so alone. I'm over it."

Blythe leaned against the tank. The red target to trigger James' seat hung above her head. She saw my eyes flick up at it, then scowled.

"I'm sorry," I said.

She sighed. "I get it. Poor James is still in peril. You

answered the question, though, so I'm keeping my word. I won't drown James."

I let go of a breath I didn't know I'd been holding. James sobbed and thanked Blythe over and over.

"Where are the stairs?" I asked.

"We won't tell anyone, Blythe," James said. "Give us a story, and we'll stick to it."

Blythe smiled at her.

James peered at me from high above, hope in her eyes.

I took a step back and searched the area for the ladder.

Blythe's smile fell. Her cheeks were sunken, her eyelids heavy. Shadows slashed across her face, making her appear demonic. Her nostrils flared, her fingers twitched.

The relief faded from James' face.

Blythe leaped toward the target. I reached out to grab her.

I missed.

Her hand hit the target, a little slap barely strong enough to trigger the seat. It dropped out from under James, who gasped as she plopped into the water.

The water fizzed and hissed like Alka-Seltzer as red clouds bloomed around James. Her mouth opened in a silent scream. It stretched wide until her cheeks split, and her lower jaw separated from her face and floated away. Her eyes, wide open in shock, melted. The skin peeled off her skull and dissipated, leaving only bone behind.

James jerked wildly. I prayed it was involuntary, the last firings of her nervous system as her body tore to pieces. The meat in her chest dissolved, her ribs appeared. Her heart, tucked between the bones, became visible for a moment before breaking into bits.

Her legs kicked, continuing to tread water unsuccessfully. One split from her torso, followed by the other. Her clothes were gone, but her shoes were inexplicably still tied to her feet. All the things stitching her body together unraveled, and the remaining chunks drifted apart.

Bloody red remnants got smaller and smaller, until they turned pink, then disappeared altogether.

Only her disassembled skeleton remained. It started to dissolve too, more slowly than her flesh.

I fell to the ground screaming.

"Why?" I begged. "You said you wouldn't kill her!"

Blythe shrugged, a bemused expression on her face.

"I said I wouldn't drown her. I didn't say a word about dropping her in acid."

CHAPTER 25

"Do you think she felt it?" Blythe asked, tapping on the glass.

I barely heard the words. The bright carnival lights twinkled around me. My screams grew louder and louder, drowning out the cheerful music from the carousel.

Blythe kicked me.

"Stop crying!" she yelled.

"Why?" I asked. "We had a deal. Why did you kill her?"

"Because her death was part of my plan. Get up."

"I can't."

She pulled me to my feet and slammed me into the dunk tank. Remnants of James' skull floated past.

I couldn't breathe. My vision blurred. As I gasped for air, I choked, then coughed, then vomited on Blythe's feet.

"Oh gross," she said, kicking the chunks off her shoes. She'd traded her heels for sensible black sneakers. "Listen to me, Violet." She took my chin and turned my face. "Do not fall down. Alright? Stay standing."

"Why did you do this?" I asked. "Don't give me some bullshit about internet views or colleges or the future."

"I'm miserable. I thought it would make me feel better," she whispered.

"Are you going to kill me too?"

She sighed. "When I first decided to do this, I planned to kill you. You're terrified of the Ferris wheel, right?"

"I don't like the Whirling Witch either. Heights freak me out."

"Yes. I figured we'd ride to the top, and I'd throw you off. I didn't want to mangle you or make you suffer. You were collateral damage, not a direct target. Then I second-guessed myself. It's been painful to watch you these past few months. How can a person be mopey and anxious at the same time? I'm shocked your hair isn't falling out. Like, how do I kill such a weak girl? You must be in as much pain as I am. Right?"

I nodded and blubbered.

"I'll take that as a yes. So I'm pathetic, you're pathetic, we're kindred spirits. A week ago, when I spent the day mapping the carnival out, I realized I had no choice. I can't be the sole survivor if you're around, and if you're around, you'll tell. Pathetic people always tell. So perfect. Too perfect."

Blythe smoothed my hair and tucked it behind my ear. She smiled, light in her eyes, her blonde hair glowing like a halo around her head. Still angelic, even covered in blood.

"Even Lucifer was an angel," I mumbled to myself.

Blythe tilted her head. "I, uh. Good? Does that mean something? Are you finding Jesus right here in this carnival or something?" She waited for me to answer. I didn't. She shook it off. "Anyway. Last week I was going to kill you. Tonight at dinner, I saw your dopey sad eyes, and I changed my mind again. I'm never this indecisive. We might not be BFFs like you and what's left of James, but I always liked you better than those other bitches. Girls. Sorry. You don't like me calling them bitches."

"I don't care anymore. Just tell me what you're going to do."

"Can't make up my mind," she said. "I've got an idea, though."

Blythe pulled her phone out.

"Who are you calling?" I asked.

"It's the only fair way to decide. Heads you win, tails you lose," she said. "Siri, Flip a coin."

Of all the insane things I'd seen that night, AI flipping a coin to seal my fate took the cake.

I held my breath.

"It's heads this time," the robotic voice announced.

"Listen to that! You win!" She reached into her pocket and pulled out a washcloth. "You win this!"

She shoved the washcloth into my face and dug her hand into my hair to hold my head in place.

She moved too fast for me to fight back.

Everything went black.

CHAPTER 26

S ixth grade.
  We met in art class.
  I couldn't draw. Blythe could.

Artists made me so jealous. There was always one kid in class who, without training, could produce a photorealistic flower bouquet or self-portrait. I'd been gifted with a musician's ears, but not with an artist's eye.

Our teacher, Ms. Daley, assigned seats. Blythe and I shared a table made for two. I wrote with my right hand, she wrote with her left. Our assigned seats made us bump elbows, so Ms. Daley permitted us to switch.

Blythe was prettier than all the other girls except Mila, even before her eventual internet celebrity makeover. She had dark hair then, and she wore braces. Her body was a jumble of sticks she hadn't yet learned to maneuver.

Her desire to be friends stunned me. I wasn't a total loser, but she was much more mature. At first, I didn't particularly enjoy hanging out with her because it triggered an (unfounded) fear that she would force me to steal a car or drink or hook up with guys. I befriended her anyway. Who doesn't want to be tight with the cool girl? Blythe was an outfit to try on, a costume to wear to impress the other kids.

One day our teacher brought a huge canvas to class. She'd painted heaven as she saw it: Serene blues, dogs with angel wings, cotton candy clouds with rainbow sprinkles.

"When I die, this is where I want to be. Puppies and candy, there's nothing better. I want you each to draw the place where you want to spend your afterlife. Is your heaven like mine? I want to be on a sunny beach with my fiancee and dozens of dogs. Perhaps you would prefer a garden, maybe a mansion? Who is in your heaven with you? What items are there?"

A girl raised her hand.

Our teacher called on her. "Eris? Do you have a question?"

"Does it have to be the same scope as yours? What if my heaven is smaller? What if it's one particular puppy instead of a puppy filled beach?"

"Excellent question. If your idea of heaven is gazing into the face of a loved one, draw the person. A word to the wise, please take this seriously. As always, we'll be doing a critique at the end, so if you draw a bowl of fruit, you need to be able to explain why you want to spend eternity with apples and bananas."

She asked if anyone else had questions. No one did, so she walked the room as everyone started their sketches.

My abilities were mediocre. I could draw simple, cartoony pictures, not so awful that you couldn't tell what I'd drawn, but bad enough that you forgot about them as soon as you moved on to the next drawing.

Music was the foundation for my heaven, so I drew musical notes to represent stars in the sky, and swirls I would later fill with a colorful rainbow to represent sound.

"Oh, yours is going to be pretty," Blythe said.

I smiled. "Thanks. What are you doing?"

She showed me her sketch paper. She'd drawn an ornate frame around the edge of the paper but had left the center blank.

"I'm lost. What should I put in the frame?"

"What do you love most?"

"Strawberry cheesecake," she joked.

I laughed. "Draw that."

"Cheesecake is what a wine mom would say. It's a cop-out." Blythe frowned at her drawing. "I accidentally drew the mirror above our dining room table."

"Does this mean your idea of heaven is staring at yourself in the mirror?"

"Who wouldn't want to stare into these Bette Davis eyes for eternity?"

I wanted to make a joke, raise my hand, and say, "Me, me!" but I couldn't risk her taking it the wrong way and thinking I didn't like her. I decided to go deep.

As deep as a thirteen-year-old can go, anyway.

"Maybe it's not your reflection. Maybe you drew a mirror because your idea of heaven is looking into the mirror and being happy with what you see?"

Blythe leaned over and drew a tiny clef note on my paper.

"You're a good egg, Violet. You get it."

She beamed. We'd had a moment, and now we were allies. My comment meant something to her; she'd finally been heard.

In reality, it wasn't some deep connection. My words only served to stroke her ego. Our moment was one-sided.

But I took it.

Who wouldn't want to be friends with a girl like Blythe?

A week later, we reported to class with our finished assignments.

In mine, streaky rainbows and uneven music notes burst from a lumpy violin's belly. Nothing fancy, easy to describe to the class, and it wouldn't draw too much attention to my lack of talent.

Blythe arrived with her painting tucked under her arm. She held it up for me to see.

She'd drawn a girl lounging in a frilly purple bedroom inside the frame. Chestnut hair framing a heart-shaped face, chin resting on long, manicured fingers. The girl had no features, blank white space instead of eyes, a nose, and a mouth.

"You didn't finish it," I said. Something about the realistic body with the missing face unsettled me. My skin crawled as I felt her watching me, despite the lack of eyes.

"I finished it. It's called *An Unfinished Portrait of Blythe*. She's not supposed to have a face."

"Why not?"

"You said it yourself. My heaven can be self-acceptance. I don't accept myself yet, though, so I don't know what that's supposed to look like."

Her explanation sounded surprisingly profound for someone our age. She made me feel like a child standing next to a woman.

"Is that really what it means?" I asked.

Blythe held her face still for a moment, and then her lips cracked into a smile.

"Uh, no. I got distracted and forgot the damn thing. I didn't have time to finish the face, so I pulled the meaning out of my ass. It's good, right? My masterpiece!"

"It's good," I said. "Even without being done. Your story sells it."

"Right? It's a trick I learned. This painting is a jumping off point. I kept it basic so that I could go over the top with the fake story. Art is subjective, so people will believe what you tell them. You need confidence."

She'd missed the entire point of the assignment unless her idea of heaven was a nap on a cloud of lies.

"What's your story going to be?" she asked.

"It's pretty music and rainbows," I said. "I don't think there *is* a story."

"Boring. It's fine, though. The whole assignment is kinda boring. It would've been way more interesting if Ms. Daley had us draw our idea of hell."

"Can teachers even say the word 'hell' in class?" I asked.

She shrugged. "This is Texas. Could go either way."

"What would you have painted?"

"Hmm. This same thing probably. I'd say, 'My idea of hell is a loss of identity.' Make shit up, say it like you believe it, make everyone else believe it too. What would you paint?"

Beyond fire and brimstone, I knew nothing about hell. I mumbled something about painting a broken violin. Blythe rolled her eyes and told me I wasn't any fun.

"Listen," I said. "My mom makes me go to church and all, but hell always seemed so far fetched. How is it right for me to rot in hell next to Hitler if shoplifting a Snickers is the worst thing I ever do? I'm not sure there is such a thing as hell. How can you draw something you don't believe in?"

"There's a famous quote," she said. "Hell is other people."

"In that case..." I took some scratch paper and sketched a terrible likeness of Blythe. I wrote her name in bubble letters and drew an arrow from the letters to the doodle.

"Oh, I'm not hell, baby," she laughed. "I'm heaven all the way."

"Hey," I grinned. "Even Lucifer was an angel."

CHAPTER 27

I regained consciousness but didn't open my eyes. I was weightless, cold. A hard metal seat was beneath me, a breeze blew my hair.

Blythe spoke at a frantic pace at full volume. Apparently, we were in the middle of a conversation, and it didn't matter to her if I was awake or not.

"You put up a fight, though, more than I expected. The candy helped so much to make you weak. I put myself through training, all the weight lifting. I told everyone it was a fitness challenge. I gained weight, but it's all muscle, so I'm skinnier than before!"

Three hard slaps made me jump. Blythe's palm slapped someone's skin.

Not mine.

I cracked my eyes a little.

I didn't want her to know I'd come around.

But when I saw the corpses sitting on the seats around me, I screamed. Blythe grabbed my face and forced her fingers past my lips, teeth, and tongue to muzzle me. I gagged until she slid her fingers out of my mouth. She wiped them on her shirt.

"You and me were having a chat, Violet. Calm down and *participate*." She put an arm around my shoulder and nodded at the bodies. "Claire, can you believe this girl? We gotta get her to chill."

Claire's skin was blue. Her clothes were filthy, covered in dirt and grass, with gravel ground into her hands. Her letterman's jacket, which she wore whether it was 40 degrees or 100, was folded in her lap.

Cotton candy completely enrobed her head: pink, fluffy, *bloody* cotton candy.

Lolly sat on the seat next to her. Or rather, Lolly's decapitated body. Her head was long gone. Maybe it was back at the test your strength booth, perhaps Blythe had hidden it for some satanic ritual later. Who knew what she was capable of at that point.

River was jammed between Lolly and the wall. Jagged circles marred her entire body, face to feet. Her eyes were open. Though her face hung slack, it retained a mask of horror. I didn't know what Blythe had done to her, but I could tell it hadn't been a pretty end.

Blythe wrapped her arm around my shoulder and gave me a squeeze. I jumped at her touch.

"You make me so proud, Violet." She said.

"You butchered them. How are you not drenched in blood?"

"I brought extra clothes."

"Of course you did. Why wouldn't you?"

Skin peeped through a hole in her black jeans, on the knee. They were probably expensive and probably came with the hole. Rich girls will pay extra to look sloppy. I poked her bare skin. She giggled.

Then her words registered.

"What do you mean you're proud?" I asked.

"Uh, look down."

A metal grate surrounded us. We were in an iron box, swinging in the air. Maybe we were fifty feet high, maybe five hundred. I'd always been terrible with measurements. I gripped the grate to steady myself. We rotated backward, locked in a gondola on the Ferris wheel.

At least I hoped we were locked in.

"Why are we up here?"

"One last ride. Check out the stars! Look at the pretty lights! Over there, on the Whirling Witch! I turned it on for us. I turned it all on."

Beneath us, the carnival was alive. The empty cars on the Whirling Witch Coaster chugged uphill, then dropped fast before flipping over in a loop. That loop kept me off the coaster. I couldn't wrap my head around the physics; I was convinced it would kill me.

Smoke poured from the House of Horrors. Robotic demonic laughter mixed with the cheerful calliope and the bleeps and sirens at the arcade. The Black Kitten Coaster went around and around on its track. The Crazy Cauldrons danced. The air smelled like Paulie's Pop-A-Corn and fresh dirt.

I pressed myself against Blythe, as though a ruthless killer might hold me tight and keep me from falling. She hugged me and smoothed my hair.

"It was hard to decide to kill you. You don't deserve it. Not like the rest of them."

"Where are the other two girls?"

"Right over there," Blythe said. She twisted in her seat and pointed to the gondola closest to ours.

Two bodies slouched over inside. Mila's bouncy curls were now flat, stringy, and sticky with blood. Gracie's head flopped forward, and her chin dipped into her gaping chest wound.

"What did you do?" I asked.

"Only one missing is James," she said, ignoring me. "There wasn't much of her left, and I'm not about to go fishing in acid for a gooey jaw bone."

"How did you even get the acid into the tank?"

"I didn't. I paid someone to smuggle it in for me. Old Ted was a terrible guard. He fell asleep at his desk a lot, and sometimes he left in the mid-shift to hit up Snowflake donuts. My guy picked the lock on the front gate and drove right in. The acid has been in there a week, waiting for James."

"Who would agree to do that for you?"

"I'm a hot underage girl on the internet. Who *wouldn't* agree to do it?"

"Gross."

"Yeah," she said, gnawing on her nail. "I didn't write the rules." She bit off the white and spit it out of the gondola. I pressed my cheek against the grate, straining to watch the fingernail fly away toward the dazzling carnival. Blythe had turned the electricity on full blast. Lights from the midway lit the dunk tank from behind, making the pale pink liquid appear neon red.

The aftermath of Blythe's spree stunned me. Our dusty footprints drew paths across the carnival; glittery broken glass sparkled in the grass. Smoke poured from under the food court awning. The arcade door hung on its hinges, and an axe was buried in the wood next to deep red handprints. Streaky blood smears stained the concrete where Blythe had dragged the bodies across the ground to hide them for her big reveal.

"It's all very impressive," I told her. I meant it. "If you told me one of my friends was going to go on a murder spree, I'd have placed my bet on Lolly. It's usually the quiet ones."

Blythe beamed. "I'm a true artiste. This is my masterpiece!"

"And you said you didn't have any talent."

"Well, I can't exactly put this all online," she said. She reached into her pocket and winked. "Or can I?"

She handed me her phone. The case was pink opal marble. She'd stuck a neon green llama sticker under the camera lens. He wore sunglasses, and River always used to say "He's a coooooooool llama friend," when Blythe whipped out her phone. She'd draw out the "o" further and further each time until she broke out into uncontrollable laughter. No one else ever found it funny, but it entertained me when River tickled herself with her dumb joke.

Blythe grabbed my wrist and twisted it around so she could use facial recognition to unlock her phone.

A photo grid filled the screen. She'd posted a collage from the night to social media, dozens and dozens of photos. I scrolled through and tapped one.

Toward the end of dinner, Blythe had given her phone to a busboy so she could take a group photo. Claire crossed her eyes and stuck out her tongue, River sat beside her with her head on Gracie's shoulder, James and I sat front and center, her fingers wrapped in mine, raised above our heads in triumph. Each girl so happy, cheesing it up.

Except for Blythe.

She stared straight into the camera, one eyebrow raised, her canine clamped on her lip. While the rest of us clumped together into a lovely mess of limbs, she stood behind us, off to the side. Danger loomed behind us, ready to grind us into mulch, and we had no idea.

The next photo was the group shot we took in the woods. Again, while the rest of us smiled, Blythe sneered.

A third photo was Mila, James, and River from behind, walking to the dark carnival, followed by a pic that looked like she'd taken it from her pocket: Gracie in profile, half obscured by black fabric.

I gasped out loud as I scrolled, freezing on Blythe, alone in a mirror selfie in the girls' bathroom. In this picture, she gave a genuine smile and flashed a peace sign. My feet were visible under a stall door in the background. Another photo in the same setup followed, but in the second one, she'd put on The Licker's mask. Instead of the peace sign, she gave the finger.

"Did you document the whole thing?"

"Duh. It's what I do. Keep going."

I pulled up the next photo, gasped, and chucked the phone at Blythe.

She'd taken a close, artsy shot of Lolly's obliterated head, and she'd posted it online.

"What is wrong with you?" I asked.

"So. Much. There's video too. Check my stories."

Blythe picked the phone up but didn't give it back. While I'd been unconscious, she'd uploaded a video. She pressed play and stuck the phone in my face, close enough for the screen to kiss my nose. I jerked back to watch the screen.

In the video, Blythe held the camera at a downward angle and positioned herself so the corpses and I were also in the shot. My body went limp, my head rolled back, resting on the metal seat. I appeared to be as dead as the others.

"Hey guys," she said. "Welcome back! I told y'all earlier I'd be offline tonight, but I have a special surprise."

Video Blythe flipped the camera around so the viewer could get a good look at River, Claire, and Lolly. She held it on River's blank eyes for a second, before turning it back to herself.

"So in case you missed my earlier videos, at my school, we have this tradition. Every year, a group of graduating Senior girls picks a group of incoming Senior girls and sets up a scavenger hunt. I was super surprised to find out I'd been picked! And all my friends got picked too! Like Violet here." She lifted her hand and patted me on the cheek. "Don't worry about her. She's having a little nap, but she's fine. The rest though… Yikes Krispies."

Video Blythe again turned the camera on the girls, straining to show the other gondolas.

"I'd like to apologize to my friends, their families, my family, my hometown, and my viewers. I made a huge mess. I made mistakes. But if you knew what I was going through, you'd understand. You see…"

I knocked the phone from her hand.

"How long did you drone on for?" I asked.

"The video is fourteen minutes and twenty-eight seconds long. I had to explain myself."

I rolled my eyes. "My name is Blythe," I said, mocking the over the top Texan accent she used on camera. "I'm a lunatic. Here are the bodies. Here is my confession. Pay attention to me."

Blythe slapped me across the face, shoved me aside, and flung the gondola door open. She threw me to the floor and kicked me so hard she knocked my head and left arm out of the gondola. I closed my eyes and prepared to fall. Blythe seized a handful of my hair and yanked me back in, locking the gondola door behind me.

"Are you really in a position to mock me?" she asked.

"Oh what are you going to do?" I asked. "Kill me?"

She shrugged. "I hadn't decided."

"Please," I said. "You decided. You decided before we even got here. You just lied to yourself and said you'd spare me so you'd feel like less of a villain. How altruistic, to save the poor girl whose future sucks maybe more than yours. Well, guess what? That's not true. Maybe I won't get into DSU. Even though I've been dramatic, it's not too late for me to apply to other schools. There are other orchestras, other ways to get where I want to go. I'm not like you. I hit a bump in the road. You're a useless asshole."

Blythe's eyes bulged. Her mouth twisted into a smile, and she clapped.

"I'd give you a standing ovation, but it would rock the gondola. I know how heights make you lose your shit."

"I'm less and less scared the longer we're up here."

"Finally! We always said you needed to jump in and go for a ride, and you'd see it wasn't bad!" Blythe gripped Claire's limp hand and used it to give herself a high five.

I scoffed. "Oh my God, why are you acting like this is a party?"

"Because this video has been online for less than half an hour, and it's already got six million views!"

She scrolled through the comments on the video, her face glowing. "'Dude, awesome effects!'" She read aloud, then turned to me. "They think it's fake! Should I be offended or flattered? Check this one, 'Always knew you were crazy, bitch! This is your best yet! Can't wait for more!'"

Other comments weren't quite as positive.

I pointed at the screen. "'You're a real sick piece of shit.'" I read aloud.

"Where's the lie? Let's check my texts."

Her entire message app lit up with blue "unread" dots.

> **DOTTIE COTTON**
>
> Are you okay?
>
> **BRIAN J - MANAGER**
>
> Is this a joke? Where are you? What did you do?
>
> **MOM**
>
> Call me. Now.
>
> **JACK BELL**
>
> I can help you. It doesn't have to end this way.
> Please call me, Blythe.
>
> **RILEY ELLIS**
>
> River isn't answering her phone. I need to talk to
> her right now. This isn't funny. Have her call me.

"Dude, that last one," Blythe said. "Riley is in for a surprise."

"You murdered her big sister."

"Eh. She attacked me with a bottle."

"Because you put on a freaky costume and stalked her."

"Whatever."

Blythe quietly read the comments, a serene smile on her face. I watched her switch back and forth between six or seven apps, examining what she'd posted on each one.

I cleared my throat.

"What?" she asked.

"What now?"

She pointed the camera at me. "Any last words?"

I stared at the lens.

"Someone will see this and call the cops. They're coming for you."

"Maybe. But they ain't gonna catch me."

"You confessed to everything and provided enough evidence to convict you ten times over. This is Texas. You're going to fry."

"No I'm not," she said. She pushed past me and opened the door again. "I'm going to *fly*."

"Are you going to jump?" I asked.

"Originally, no. When I decided you should die - and yes, I did just decide it, I never really knew - it needed to be clean. I don't have it in me to mutilate you. Future plans aside, you're different from them. You have to die, but you don't have to slasher movie die. I wasn't going to put all of this online. I couldn't help myself. It's better to go out with a bang, right?"

I couldn't listen to her anymore. A hot, orange sun peeked over the horizon. No cops had arrived to rescue me. If I intended to walk out alive, it was now or never.

I took her phone and threw it out the open door. We watched it hit a beam, bounce off, and fall to the ground.

"Guess this is it," she said.

I nodded. "Guess so." Blythe was much stronger than I expected. Her arms felt hard and tight; she pinned me to my seat without breaking a sweat. "You really have been working out," I said.

She lifted my shoulders and smacked me backward, causing my head to bang against the grate. I saw stars. I wrapped my fingers around her biceps and pinched the skin.

"Whoa, your fingers are rough!" she said, her jaw locked.

She wasn't wrong. Years of playing the violin had left me with sandpaper fingertips.

I let go of her arm and jammed my thumb in her eye. She screeched.

"Too rough for you?"

"Little bitch," she grunted. She pulled my index finger back to pry my hand from her face. The joint cracked, her eyes bulged. "I'm so sorry, Violet. I can't help myself."

Blythe rammed my hand into the door frame. It hurt, but no worse than stubbing a toe or hitting my funny bone. She grunted and kept a tight grip on my wrist, refusing to let me pull away. A smile stretched across her face as she closed my hand in the door. I screamed; Blythe cackled as she opened the door, then banged it shut a second time. Inhuman sounds came from my mouth as I tried to wiggle my fingers. I managed to fold my middle, ring, and pinky back, but I couldn't bend my index finger. I couldn't even *feel* my index finger.

I gulped for air. "Stop."

"I lied, Violet. I'm not going to do it."

"Please," I begged. I knew what she intended to do before she did it.

"I'm not going to kill you. I'm just going to end your life."

Blythe screwed her face up, opened the door wide, and slammed it on my finger with every ounce of strength she possessed. As I lay on the ground, thrashing and panicking, Blythe kicked my arm back into the gondola and dropped my hand onto my chest. My index finger was almost completely severed. Blood gushed everywhere; it poured on my face, my torso, the floor, and River's shoes. One remaining sliver of skin held the finger on my hand.

I couldn't watch when she wrapped it in her hand and plucked it like a flower petal.

She loved me not, so she pitched it over her shoulder. It flew through the grate, landing God knows where.

"I can't have you bleed to death," she said. Lolly's t-shirt was shredded, so Blythe ripped off a few pieces of fabric and tightened them on my hand. She could do as she pleased; I went numb, unable to process what she'd done. Satisfied with her work, she sat next to me and pulled her knees to her chest. "Nobody ever becomes a professional musician anyway. You'll probably become an accountant or something. I helped you cut to the chase." She paused, leaning forward, waiting for me to reply.

But there were no words.

My heartbeat hummed in my ears. Cold blue static clouded my vision. My breath quickened, coming in random bursts. Blue static became hot, white light. Rage simmered in my chest.

Fuck. This. Whore.

I lifted my feet and kicked them into her pretty face. She flailed wildly, grasping for me, but instead pulled Claire's body onto her own. The cotton candy got in her mouth. She frantically spat it out.

"It's like licking copper pipes covered in sand," she yelled. "And this bitch is crushing me!"

Blythe squirmed away from Claire and grabbed a rail on the ceiling to pull herself to her feet. As she stood, the gondola swung.

I should've panicked. My body trembled; I'd lost too much blood. We'd made it to the top of the Ferris wheel. It jolted as it locked in place so we could take in the view. One glance toward the ground and I would've lost my mind. Fortunately, my fury kept me focused. Though my legs shook and my blood-drenched hands slipped on the wall around me, I dragged myself to my feet and reached for a rail above.

"What are you gonna do?" she asked.

"This."

I gripped the rail and rocked my body back. The gondola rocked, this time harder. My sneakers slipped in Claire's blood, but I didn't fall. I used the momentum of the gondola to rock it again. This time it swung backward and rattled sideways.

"Stop it!" Blythe screamed. "You're going to kill us both!"

"So are you!"

"Yeah, but I earned it!"

"Crazy bitch," I mumbled as I hit the wall.

Blythe dove for me, claws out, ready to wrap around my neck.

Before she could catch me, she tripped over Claire's body. She flopped face-first at my feet. She strained to raise her head.

Her nose gushed blood; one front tooth held on by a thread.

"Too bad your phone's gone. Your fans would die if they could see you now."

Blythe coughed, choking on blood.

"*You* could die," she said sarcastically.

"Not today."

Blythe struggled to get to her feet. The adrenaline had begun to wear off, and the injuries she'd sustained while playing psycho killer had caught up to her. The gondola swung, threatening to knock her over again. She lifted her head high and smiled.

Her tooth fell out. She didn't even flinch.

"I was never going to walk away from this," she said.

"I know," I whispered. "Please don't make me do it."

"Yeah. You don't need that. I've already given you enough therapy material for the next thirty years."

"Forty."

"Glad I made an impression."

Silver light shone through the grate, casting square shadows on her face. Tiny cotton candy strands clung to her chin. My blood coated her hands. Her clothes were ribbons, and she stank like pickle juice. She closed her eyes and took a deep breath.

Even after everything she'd done, I didn't want her to destroy herself.

"What about Europe?" I asked, interrupting the cinematic suicide moment playing out in her head.

"What?" she whispered.

"In the car. You said I could be your intern. Why say it if you were going to do this?"

"Wishful thinking." She stared dreamily at the Whirling Witch Coaster. "One last chance to give myself an out. But the lights never lie. Those miles and miles of flashing red traffic lights, they told me I should follow through. Ya gotta listen to the lights."

Blythe glanced over her shoulder, her chest heaving as the gravity of the situation sank in. She turned back and gave me a little wave.

I waved back with my ruined hand.

At first, I thought she would elegantly fall backward, drifting into the air, eyes closed, peaceful. Instead, she turned to face the world, raised her hands above her head, and swan dived into the pinkish gray light of dawn. Though I couldn't stomach watching her final descent, her screams echoed in my ears. They ended abruptly when her body crunched as it hit the metal gears at the bottom of the ride.

I closed the gondola door and waited for the wheel to spin me to freedom. It had been rigged to turn infinitely. When the gondola got low enough, I leapt to the ground. I landed on my side, ribs bruised but unbroken.

Blythe's body was sprawled out, butter side down, hair spread out, obscuring her face. I tried not to look; I was mostly successful.

A pile of junk lay at the Ferris wheel ticket stand. She'd left her backpack, The Licker's mask and cloak, a hunting knife, and James' jacket behind. I slipped my arms into the jacket and dug through the backpack to find her key fob, which I stuck in my pocket and stumbled away.

I'd taken about six steps when I paused, went back to the stand, snatched a paper fast-pass, and dragged myself to the exit.

"Who buys a white Tesla with a white interior?" I asked out loud as I fumbled around with the seat placement. Trails of my bloody fingerprints spotted the car, from the door to the wheel. My remaining fingers stuck to the white leather. I squeezed the wheel and released several times until it was less tacky to the touch.

I'd had my license for nearly two years but rarely used it.

James always drove us everywhere.

My heart leapt into my throat. I swallowed hard, refusing to cry.

Police sirens wailed as they sped toward the carnival. I watched through the trees as ten or fifteen cop cars swarmed the parking lot, followed by a pair of fire trucks. They would bombard me with questions, and I needed to process the events before I could handle an inquisition. Plus, I had a pancake breakfast to attend, and I didn't want to keep the girls waiting.

I put the car in reverse and managed to drive away, unseen.

CHAPTER 28

My brain recorded no memories from my drive. When it clicked back on, I found myself in the parking lot of the Crave Inn. Only a handful of other cars were parked around me. A neon sign blinked in the window, promising pizza. I stretched against the wheel like a prairie dog to see a few familiar heads of hair inside the restaurant.

When I walked in, the hostess gasped. Every patron turned to stare. The cook burst from the kitchen with an oversized whisk in hand, his mouth a gaping O. Gloopy batter dripped off the whisk and onto a woman dining on a large Belgian waffle.

I caught a glimpse of myself in the glass door. My nude bra peeped out from a boob sized hole in my shirt. I closed James' jacket and hugged myself. For a second, I was embarrassed I'd flashed the room, totally forgetting that I was also drenched in blood and covered in bruises. My shoe had come untied. I bent over to tie it and found a cotton candy fluff stuck to the toe.

"Violet?" asked a familiar voice softly. "Are you okay?"

Maddy Bryant, my friend, the person whose innocent invitation doomed me to a night of terror, stood over me, shaking. She wore a faded teal t-shirt with a circular logo on the chest. The words "I survived the Pritchett High Senior Scavenge

2019" wrapped around the logo. A goofy peacock shot finger guns at me from the center. Maddy had another shirt in her hand. She helped me remove the jacket and pulled the fresh shirt over my head. I immediately put the jacket back on.

My shirt was a variant of Maddy's. It read, "I survived the Pritchett High Senior Scavenge 2020." Instead of finger guns, my peacock wore a clown costume and brandished a cotton candy cone.

More girls in teal 2019 t-shirts surrounded me, each one making the same slack-jawed face as the cook.

A chorus of voices assaulted me with questions.

"What happened to you?"

"Should we take you to the ER? Somebody call 911!"

"Where are the other girls?"

"Is this a joke? Please tell me this is a joke."

I reached under the hostess stand, snatched a menu, and flipped through the pages.

"Pecan pancakes might be tradition, but I think I'd prefer cranberry orange with a scoop of Blue Bell," I told no one in particular. "Homemade Vanilla flavor for sure."

Maddy slid into the chair next to me. She placed a hand on my back and rubbed small circles.

"Violet, can you please acknowledge us?"

I put the menu on the table and stared deep into her eyes.

"I acknowledge you," I said. I turned to the other girls. "Seems like y'all haven't been online. Check Blythe's social media. Go fast before they delete it."

Everyone pulled out their phones. Within seconds, I death screams poured from the speakers. Gasps from the girls around me overpowered them.

The waitress stopped by the table to refill the water glasses. She eyeballed me up and down, then turned on her heels to walk away. I stopped her and asked for chocolate milk. She nodded, eyes wild.

"This is real?" asked Maddy.

"Very," I said. I stole Delilah Cortez's water and chugged the entire glass. She owed me. She was the one who'd invited Blythe to the Scavenge.

"Everyone is dead?" Delilah asked.

I nodded. "Turns out Blythe was a little uncertain about her future after high school, so she chose to channel her fear into an evening of mayhem and murder." I looked around me. Eight blank faces stared back. "Yes. Everyone is dead. Blythe was nuts. Have you guys ordered yet?"

Blue and red lights flashed outside. Two police cruisers and an ambulance had arrived.

I took another glass of water and gulped until it froze in my chest. "I guess that's my ride," I said.

I stood and squeezed past Maddy. Before I could leave, she grabbed my wrist.

"I'll call your mom, and we'll meet you at the hospital," she said. "But you should take this. It's yours."

Maddy handed me a rough, weighty envelope. My name and address were scrawled on the outside in crisp calligraphy.

"Where did you get this?" I asked.

"Your mom called me last night. It came in the mail while you were in Austin with James. She didn't want to interrupt the Scavenge, so she had me pick it up. She wanted it to be a surprise."

I turned the envelope over. A bloody thumbprint stained the flap, right next to the official wax seal of Desert Springs University. I snapped the seal, opening it.

I read the words written on the canvas three or four times, absorbing next to nothing, but managing to get the gist.

"What does it say?" asked Maddy.

"I got in."

ALSO BY IVY THOLEN

Tastes Like Candy 2: Sugarless

Maul Rats: A Slasher Novel

Mother Dear: A Slasher Novel

Available at Amazon

Join Ivy's Mailing List for Updates on Future Releases at
www.ivytholen.com

ABOUT THE AUTHOR

Ivy Tholen is the author of the *Tastes Like Candy* series, *Maul Rats*, and *Mother Dear*.

She prefers blue cotton candy.

Visit her at www.ivytholen.com

instagram.com/ivy_tholen

amazon.com/author/ivy-tholen